Slowed by a Baby

An African Woman's Journey ~ Book 2

Eileen K. Omosa

Copyright

Slowed by a Baby: An African Woman's Journey ~ Book 2

The book is a work of fiction. The characters, names, settings, incidents, and dialogues are all products of the author's imagination or used fictitiously. Locales and public names are sometimes used for atmospheric purposes Any resemblance to actual events, business establishments or persons, living or dead, is entirely coincidental. The author acknowledges the trademarked status and trademark owners of the various products referenced in this work of fiction. There are no affiliated gains associated with their use at this time.

Each of the books can be read as a standalone or part of a series. Some of the characters in one book are found in earlier or future books in the series.

Thank you in advance for telling your family, friends, and colleagues about this book.

Eileen K. Omosa/We Grow Ideas
Slowed by a Baby
Published, 2019
Canada
ISBN: 9781999182816
www.eileenomosa.com

Acknowledgements

I am grateful to every individual consulted while I went about creating *Slowed by a Baby.* The following people made a professional contribution:

Copy editor: Ken Amuaya

Cover design: cathyscovers.wix.com/books

Wardrobe editor: Darleen Masakhwe

Logistics: Eugene Wambongo

Book design template by BookDesignTemplates.com

DEDICATION

To all the girls and women making decisions and choices during unpredictable times. Through sheer effort, you prove to society that positive change is possible.

Synopsis

His wife staying in employment will reflect on his capability, but resigning from her job will stall her career growth. Will they ever find a middle ground?

In less than two years, Sophia has hauled her family out of poverty. Satisfied with the outcome of her hard work, she's focused on building a career with a stable income when Richie asks her to resign from her job and become a stay-at-home-mom.

Sophia cannot imagine life without her job, the way to realize her career dreams.

Richie cannot envision his wife struggling to balance the tasks of wife, mother, and employee. He prefers she stays at home, provide the comfort he needs to succeed at his job and provide for financial needs of his family.

How will Richie convince Sophia that he has enough wealth for his wife not to work a single day, yet Sophia is determined to prove that a woman can balance her professional and family life?

CONTENTS

Chapter 1

Richie Mwasimba jolted out of his chair and hurried out of the office. He needed to see Sophia to appease his mind, the only way he could then focus on the time-bound document on his computer screen.

Determined to be promoted into the position of director, he was fully aware that could only happen through hard work to turn the idea from his father into reality, a new department.

Richie moved with a gait wished for by many of his age-mates. His well-trimmed black hair and clean-shaven face concealed the troubling thoughts clouding his mind that morning.

Taking long strides towards the east wing of Akoth Towers, he knew that he was about to break a rule he had made–a promise to Sophia that the only time he would visit her office was to consult on work-related matters.

He knocked on her door, like it hurt his knuckles. Hesitated for a moment, then pressed the handle and walked inside.

Sophia looked up and saw the person she least expected, her husband. From her seated position, Richie, in a black Armani pinstriped suit, appeared taller than his six-foot one inch.

Distracted by his unexpected arrival, she smiled, revealing the full depth of the dimples on her heart-shaped face. Her hands went to her head and smoothed her braids upwards, as if making sure the braids pinned to the top of her head were still intact.

She rolled her chair backwards and stood up as he reached her desk. He stretched his sturdy chest across the mahogany desk to reach her, without success. With smiley eyes, he held her left hand to his mouth and kissed the back of her slender fingers.

Sophia pointed him to one of the visitor chairs in front of her desk. "Nice to see you, please make yourself comfortable," she welcomed him, supposing nothing other than work-related issues had brought him into her office before nine in the morning.

Revealing his long well-arranged white teeth, he made eye contact with her. "Thanks, Sunshine. I will not be here for long, I missed you." He sat on the visitor chair as he glanced at the door connecting Sophia and Michael's offices.

She chuckled as her oval eyes sank deeper under her eyelids, revealed her laugh lines. "Now, now, I see someone losing their managerial position for missing his wife, a wife busy with her office tasks." She tilted her chin towards Michael's office. "How will people interpret that?"

With both arms resting on her desk, he gawked and leaned more towards her and spoke in a muffled voice,

"How nice it would be for both of us not to leave the north wing, no need to hurry out of bed to get to work."

The smile faded from her face as her eyes widened. "The best part is that I am not about to lose my PA post, which means you will stay in bed while I come to work."

Noticing how serious she appeared, her eyebrows pulled in, he held back the laughter threatening to escape from his mouth, though his cheery eyes betrayed him.

She asked, "Are you aware of our upcoming trip? Will you come with us to Rwanda?"

Richie frowned as his dark-grey chiseled face went a shade darker, at her mention of the trip.

Realizing Sophia had detected his strained facial expression, he said, "I wish it was a trip to Italy with you..." He sat upright, pushing his shoulders back and chest forward, "Back to that hotel room of last year."

He watched as her face brightened up, he guessed that his statement had reminded her of their official trip to Rome, six months before their wedding.

Upon her mentioning the trip to Rwanda, Richie had wanted to ask if she would still travel all over the world for work, as she did before their marriage. How he wished to let her know of his desire, that she resign from her job and stay home. That way, she would give the support he needed to put more effort into his managerial, and soon to be director of a department.

According to his plans, if Sophia stayed home, he would be the only one hurrying out of the house each morning, and the only one tired at the end of each workday. Unlike when they both arrive home tired.

He also worried about what his family members, friends and co-workers would think of him if Sophia did not resign. That, he was not working hard enough, earn enough money to release his wife from the arduous world of employment.

He stood up and startled Sophia who had been staring at him. He walked around the desk and stood behind her as she turned in his direction. "No spying on the PA computer, Michael will punish both of us."

Sophia worked as a personal assistant to Michael Mwasimba, the Director of Marketing.

"Would you believe it if I told you that my mind is too preoccupied to register whatever is on that screen?" He asked as he leaned forward, held her face between his hands and kissed her before he walked away.

He paused at the door and said, "Sorry, I broke my promise. Please prod me to follow you home at the end of your workday." He winked at her, opened the door, and stepped out of her office.

She stared until the door came to a complete close.

Chapter 2

Sophia stood up and gently smoothed the pleats of her Issey Miyake midi skirt. She sat back and spell-checked the report she had been working on. Satisfied with her output, she emailed the document to Michael.

Almost reflexively, she went to the women's washroom where she checked her face in a mirror, washed her hands, and checked her face again. She was thoughtful, recalling the sad expression on Richie's face when she had mentioned her upcoming travel to Rwanda.

Next, she reflected on the many occasions when Richie had asked her to resign from her job. Her response had remained the same, that she liked her job, and preferred to remain in employment.

Other than the considerable money she earned, Sophia cherished that her knowledge in finance and business management was applicable to the goals of her employer, the Mwasimba Group of Companies.

While her PA duties involved reading and analyzing documents, and accompanying Michael to official meetings, she had never stopped updating herself on developments in the world of finance and money markets.

Subsequently, her knowledge on global financial markets had never ceased to fascinate and challenge Richie since their days at university, though he was an equally competent student.

Sophia had avoided telling Richie how frightened she became whenever the thought of being unemployed crossed her mind – it brought back memories of the poverty her family had endured, before the Mwasimba Group of Companies employed her.

Resigning from her job was tantamount to going back to the time when Mariko, her father, had been in unfathomable debt, with her siblings out of school most of the year due to lack of school fees.

Earnings from her PA job had lifted her family from below the poverty line, and ensured her brothers were back in school fulltime. Joy, her sister had consequently completed her degree program in design, while Silas, Joy's follower, was now in university pursuing a degree in mechanical engineering.

Mariko's life had transformed. He was now the owner of a profitable grocery store in the village, Mariko & Family Stores.

Sophia yanked some tissue paper from a nearby box and wiped out some of her eyeshadow. She reflected on the time she had mentioned her need for an internal transfer after Richie had asked when she would resign from her position. Instead, Richie had made it clear, if she insisted on staying in employment, she had to continue in her position as PA to Michael, his eldest brother.

A click, click sound made by quick short steps caught Sophia's attention. The thud came to an abrupt stop along the corridor before the door opened and one of the managers in the marketing department stepped inside. She paused long enough to exchange greetings with Sophia before proceeding to the furthest toilet cubicle.

Sophia turned her eyes back to the mirror while she pondered what her life would be like if she resigned from her job. She would have no salary, and no money of her own.

She washed and dried her hands, opened the door, and walked out with one wish, that her thoughts on being unemployed would remain in the washroom.

As she walked to her office, her mind was occupied with Richie's request that she quit her job. Tilting her chin slightly upwards, her mind wandered to the subtle florescent light peeping out of the lofty ceilings. How she wished to have a two-minute break between the cushioned chairs in the waiting lounge of the east wing, with its large glass windows that displayed an outside view of greenery, offering a reflexive therapy.

Sophia approached the solid mahogany reception desk at one end of the waiting lounge.

Liz, the floor receptionist made eye contact with Sophia. "Oh, I thought you had followed your husband to his office, he did not look happy when he walked by here."

"He is missing his wife. He will be okay soon," Sophia said without breaking the eye contact.

Liz exposed more of her sparkly teeth, a sign of frequent visits to a dental hygienist. "If I were you guys, I would stop for the day," she said as she glanced at her computer screen, attracted by a ping indicating a new message.

She turned her attention back to Sophia, "Does he still have access to his former residence?" she asked as she tilted her chin upwards, to indicate the topmost floor of Akoth Towers, where Richie had lived and only moved out after he married Sophia.

Sophia glared, "See you another time. I have more important work waiting at my desk." She walked away, not wanting Liz to see the irritation her statement had caused to Sophia.

Liz, who was Sophia's junior in age by one year, worked as the floor receptionist of the marketing department.

A graduate in human resources management, Liz had turned down a job offer to work in the busy Human Resource Department at the Mwasimba Group of Companies. She preferred the less demanding tasks of floor receptionist, fully aware that the receptionists on the ground floor of Akoth Towers took care of most of the work of answering telephone calls and vetting visitors before they arrived at her floor.

Putting in too much effort at the office was not one of Liz's favourite ways to pass time.

Chapter 3

The *kring, kring, kring* sound stopped as Richie neared his desk. He hesitated just long enough for his mind to register the caller ID. He spun his chair around and heaved himself onto the soft Portuguese leather before lifting the phone receiver and hitting the redial button.

He replaced the receiver after one ring. As soon as the receiver hit its resting place, the *kring, kring, kring* sound from the phone disrupted the quiet in his office once more.

He shot out of his chair and paced the room until the ringing stopped. He was reluctant to answer the phone, still undecided on whether he should buy a house or not.

Sophia had become adamant that they move out of the north wing of his parents' house, to their own residence. Each time he wanted to fulfil her aspiration, he felt apprehensive about whether she would in return agree to resign from her job and stay at home – his version of a happy family life.

One glance at his Rolex got him worried. It was now nine o'clock, two hours since he arrived in the office to finalize a report that was due in two days.

It was already Wednesday, and he was scheduled to make a presentation on Friday. It was imperative that he convinces the company directors of the need for a new department to monitor global financial markets. Yet, all he had done was puzzle over how to persuade Sophia to resign from her job.

His brow pulled in as his eyes fell on the cell phone resting on one end of his desk, obstructing the lower half of a framed photo of him and his wife, cuddled. He picked up the cell phone and shoved it into the first drawer of his desk.

He stared at the desk phone, pondering whether he should pull out the cable connecting the headset to the telephone line. The phone had become a constant reminder of his need to call the real estate agent.

Richie had done his research, reducing his lengthy list of city suburbs where they could reside, from a dozen, to five, then to two. He had already decided that Sophia would be delighted with his choice of a house in one of the leafy residential suburbs of Nairobi.

He swiveled his chair to face the panel of windows forming one wall of his office and stood up as he massaged the back of his neck. His eyes roamed over the shorter buildings next to Akoth Towers, to the faraway trees, full of green leaves watered by the March/April long rains.

He wished he could stop worrying about Sophia's desire to move from his parents' house, and instead focus on finishing the half-done presentation on his computer.

The need to convince the company directors to approve funds for the proposed department was pivotal to him. A new department meant he could work his way up from his current position of a manager to a director.

He tapped on one side of the window frame while considering the benefits associated with being director of a department at the Mwasimba Group of Companies. He would earn enough money to support the financial needs of his wife and the three children they planned to have.

Thinking of children, he made a mental note to discuss with Sophia when to start a family. He sighed before he walked back to his chair and looked at the computer screen. But his mind was far away, wondering what to tell Sophia if she mentioned the topic of moving out of his parents' house?

Dragging himself out of the chair again, he went to a bookshelf at one side of his office, though he had no need for a book. His mind was occupied with thoughts of Sophia, his wife of two months.

He reflected on the promise he had made long before he married that he would not only be a loving husband and father, but the financial provider for his family. Taking up the full monetary responsibility would release his wife from having to be employed, into their home, just like his father and older brothers had done – their wives were not in employment.

Richie was aware that Sophia loved her job and the idea of working hard to earn money. She had made it clear to him that she wanted to contribute to their financial needs as a couple. Therefore, Richie was aware that asking her to resign from her PA position would be a challenging task. He put back a book he had removed from the shelf without opening a single page.

He was surprised that a matter which had initially appeared easy to implement was now consuming much of his time at work.

A new thought brought a smirk to his face. Unlike most twenty-six-year-olds in the city, whose problem would be lack of money to rent a house, his challenge was what type of house to purchase and how to convince his wife to resign from her job.

~~~~~~~

The connecting door closed as Sophia entered her office. The door reopened, and Michael strode back in. "Thanks for the summary," he waved the papers in his hand. "There are a few changes to be made," he said as he went and sat by a small round table at one corner of Sophia's office.

Sophia followed him and sat on a chair opposite from his, surprised to see that within the brief time she had spent at the washroom, Michael had printed, read and red-marked some parts on the six-page document. She straightened the collar of her skirt-suit jacket and looked at him, listening while he explained the changes to be made in the document.
~~~~~~~

When they finished reviewing the document, Michael stood to his full height of six-foot three clad in a designer grey suit. "What's your plan for tomorrow? Do we meet here and travel together, or do we each proceed to the meeting at Two Hills?"

Sophia tilted her head upwards, her eyes focused on the ceiling while patting her cheek with her index finger. "Being an early morning meeting, let's meet at the venue." She turned her eyes back to Michael. "I hope that will be okay with you," she said while she walked towards her desk.

"I am okay with that. How is your daily travel to the office, now that you reside much farther from the city center?"

"I'm still learning, adapting. I will soon be back to my normal time, arriving earlier than eight o'clock," she said as she wheeled her chair to one side and lowered her sixty-one kilograms onto the soft leather.

"No need to struggle." He chuckled. "I can imagine the many adjustments you are having to make," he completed the sentence as he walked into his office and pulled the door behind him.

Sophia chuckled as she punched in a password to access her computer screen before she picked the marked document and started inserting the corrections. She flipped the paper to page two as she heard a message drop into her cell phone. She retrieved the phone from a drawer and read, "Sunshine, what did you do to me today? I miss you."

Her face beamed with a smile as she typed a response. "Sounds like you need an early break. Go to the restaurant with Patty" She clicked send and turned to the next red mark on the paper as another message arrived.

"Only you can help, not my cousin."

"Are you for another holiday, barely two months after our honeymoon?" She clicked send, picked up the receiver of her desk phone and dialed Richie's extension.

The first thing she noted in his voice was the lack of his usual enthusiasm, so she asked, "Are you unwell? Do you need to see a doctor, or will an early break do you some good?"

"A break might be worse. Remember, I have a presentation to make on Friday?"

"Okay. What if you go home, rest, and return to work later in the day?"

"Going home will land me uncalled for questions from Mum. You know how she worries if one of us is not as happy as she expects?"

"Good reason for us to move to our house, that way, you would go home and have a good rest without worrying about questions from Mum."

"Is it okay if we shelve that topic of a house until at least the weekend, or the week after?"

Sophia reckoned that if Richie was to complete his presentation, then her mention of their relocation had sucked up whatever energy he had left. "I will give you four weeks."

She regretted her offer as soon as the words left her mouth. She tilted her head upwards, like she was in search of divine intervention. Why had she offered a whole month, instead of the few days Richie had asked?

"You give me so many reasons to keep missing you." He followed the words with a smooching noise. "Was that good enough, or should I come over to thank you?"

"I got it. Please focus on your work task." She ended the call and continued to input revisions from the corrected document which she had held in her left hand all that time.

Chapter 4

At five o'clock Sophia received a message from Richie. "My afternoon turned the right way up. One more hour and I will chauffeur my wife to where she belongs."

Her cheeks dimpled as her face beamed with a smile. She typed a response, "Thanks for that enticing offer, but I will use office transport as I have formal documents for a meeting tomorrow morning. See you soon."

Sophia pressed a button on her desk phone to alert a driver that she was on her way to the parking garage before she left her office, wheeling a leather bag beside her. At the elevator, she saw Patty hurrying her direction, arriving just as the elevator stopped and announced, "52nd floor, going down."

Patty jumped inside the elevator, turned, and stared at Sophia as she wheeled the bag inside. Patty pressed "parking" on the elevator buttons before making eye contact with Sophia. "Newlyweds do not carry office work home. That is a no, no."

"Stop feeling so good, where's your homework?"

"I will initiate a campaign for a new regulation, just for you," she said as she pointed her index finger at Sophia.

Sophia held Patty's finger and guided it away from her face. "My husband is busy with his office work, and he will not know of this bag unless you alert him."

Patty locked eyes with Sophia, which was easy as they were of similar height. "What's up with work and bags? What are you up to this weekend? We need to meet, just the two of us. I need to hear details of your honeymoon which you have refused to share. How's life?" Patty asked the many questions in one breath.

"Life gets better by the day," Sophia said with a chuckle. "What else would you expect from your cousin?" She stretched a hand and gently poked Patty's shoulder. "He's as loving as ever. Details of our honeymoon are to remain with only me, in my heart."

Patty laughed loudly. "Keep those details with your husband, though I see they are already escaping, making your face smoother." Her eyes darted to the elevator floor-reader before she turned back to Sophia, "Did you change your facial regiment already?"

Sophia involuntarily touched her face while smiling, though she would have been annoyed if the comment had come from anyone else other than Patty. Sophia knew the words were not meant to hurt her.

Patty had been Sophia's friend since her second week of employment at the company. Though Sophia would never confess it, she had observed Patty whenever they ate together, picking tips on how to eat at prestigious eateries.

Their friendship had strengthened long before Sophia discovered that Patty and Richie were first cousins and close friends. She turned to Patty, "I am afraid if I narrate details of our honeymoon, the good feeling will escape from my heart. That means no story for you, as I have told you many times before."

Patty softly poked Sophia on the chest. "You have lost a chance. I will ask Richie for the answer, though his vivid details make me uncomfortable."

Sophia's eyes widened, like they would pop out of their oval-shaped sockets.

Patty broke into loud laughter before she said, "Are you ready for a girl-to-girl talk, or do you still prefer leaving all the storytelling to your husband?"

The elevator came to a stop and the twosome stepped out as Patty leaned closer to Sophia's ear and whispered, "I am asking about the honeymoon for myself. Since your wedding day the aunties have been on my case. Richie is my junior by very many months."

"Serves you right," Sophia joked.

Patty whispered, "I need someone to convince me that going on a honeymoon is the right thing to do."

Sophia took one step back, letting the office bag stand on its wheels before she held Patty's hands at arm-length and said, "Sounds like we will drink lots of tea. Saturday afternoon is good. Will you come over or—"

Patty interjected, "I will come over to the house, and we'll find a quiet place for girl talk." She spread out both arms and embraced Sophia, then walked away, towards her car.

Sophia walked a few steps in the opposite direction and greeted Elvin as he received the office bag from her before she climbed into the car whose door was already open for her.

Elvin, about sixty-seven years of age was a senior driver in the company. He had started as a driver to the Mwasimba family where he used to chauffeur the children to and from school. He now worked as the senior driver, mostly entrusted to drive family members who worked at Akoth Towers.

He got into the driver's seat while asking, "Is Richie joining us?"

She shook her head. "He is delayed at work. He will travel later."

"That means we can leave now?" Elvin asked as he started the engine and drove out of the basement parking of Akoth Towers, a 55-storey dark-glass building in the city center of Nairobi. The magnificent building was used by many as a landmark and direction reference point.

Elvin maneuvered through the evening traffic onto the busy University Way and merged into the stretch of vehicles on Uhuru Highway.

Sophia sat at the back of the Mercedes Benz, enjoying the soft classical music emanating from the concealed speakers.

As they waited in the slow-moving traffic, she was thoughtful, trying to guess what could have been worrying Richie that morning. She resolved that the way to figure that out was to be jovial throughout the evening and night. Her happy mood would help clear his anxiety and make him voice whatever was disturbing him.

Next, she reflected on how hard the Mwasimba sons worked, putting in more hours at work than most employees did. A frown replaced her smile as she recalled a common narrative along the city streets – that, children of rich people did not work hard, all they did was spend the wealth of their rich parents.

Sophia wished for an occasion to correct such beliefs and opinions. According to her, though poor people like her father worked hard but yielded fewer returns, some rich people worked extremely hard. She mulled over what it was that kept two equally hard-working people—the rich and poor, worlds apart in terms of money and other assets.

She lifted a hand to cover her mouth, rather, the smile threatening to break into laughter, as she remembered what Patty had shared about her fear of getting married.

Sophia was delighted that Patty had changed her views on men and was considering marriage. She smiled as she recalled that less than a year ago, she herself had held similar views, afraid of marriage - even of romance. Her argument had been that love and romance were invented to derail women from working hard and getting ahead in the public domain. She had vowed not to let romance distract her, yet here she was, married to Richie and liking her married life. She would encourage Patty to get married.

She looked forward to Saturday afternoon to share whatever information Patty would need to decide on marrying the man to whom she was engaged. Sophia was aware Patty would ask very private questions about her honeymoon, and her life as a newly married woman. Sophia resolved that she would spend Saturday morning reflecting on potential questions and how to answer them without offending Patty, though she could not recall a time when she had ever seen Patty unhappy.

The car came to a complete stop, alerting Sophia they had arrived home. She thanked Elvin and walked towards the house as she heard Elvin remind her of the bag in the car.

"Thanks, Elvin. I almost forgot about the bag. I will need it for a meeting tomorrow morning." She rubbed her left eye. "Do you know who will pick me up in the morning? I need to be at Two Hills at eight for an eight-thirty meeting."

"Okay. I will be here so that we leave at seven-thirty," Elvin said as he carried the bag to the main door where he handed it to Teresa, the senior employee among the house workers.

Sophia waved a good evening to Elvin as she walked into the house, happy that she could now strategize how to welcome Richie on his return home.

Chapter 5

Sophia paused in the kitchen and greeted Patience, her mother-in-law, before she proceeded towards the north wing of the house.

She entered their bedroom, one of the four on that side of the house. Upon entry, she stood on her toes and swirled round for a 360-degree view of the room, as though she was seeing it for the first time, the room she had slept in for sixty nights.

Humming a song on God's love for the world, she sat on a two-seater sofa along the wall next to the door from where she admired their queen-size bed, donned in a brown and lime-green bedcover with matching pillows.

The bed was right in front of her view, at the far end of the opposite wall. She shifted her eyes to the left side, letting them fall beyond the dresser table, to the sheer-draped panel of glass windows.

She went closer to one of the windows from where she had a better view of the neatly cut live fence a couple of meters from the veranda outside the bedroom.

She lifted her right hand onto her chest for no obvious reason other than gratitude, that she was now part of an endowed family, resident in a serene environment in the city. No noise from passing vehicles.

The Mwasimba palatial home in Karen was located at the far end of a private driveway, off a public road.

Sophia walked the length of the wall, stopping to unhook curtain holders, freeing the cotton-lined silk window drapes. She blocked out the African sunset streaming into the room before she walked the direction of the door, turned left, past the walk-in wardrobe and opened the bathroom door.

Thirty minutes later, Sophia had bathed and changed into casual clothes, a floral cotton umbrella skirt that reached just above her knees and a plain cream blouse. She left the bedroom and walked across the family room, and into the smaller dining room. She stepped into the kitchen with an excuse, "Sorry I am late. I wanted to be here as you start cooking the main dish for dinner," she said while looking at Patience.

Richie's mother rarely missed taking charge of the food preparation whenever she was home, which was often. Though she always had two people in the kitchen, a house chef and a cleaner, she liked to cook for her family. Having spent most of her married life as a stay-at-home mom, she was accustomed to working alongside her staff, both within and outside of the house.

Patience got married to Mwasimba at the age of twenty and worked as a teacher until Bill, her third child was born. Mwasimba then requested her to stay home and take care of the family, since he worked long hours to build the family business. This was his way of ensuring that their children grew up with at least one parent at home.

By staying home to take care of the children, Patience enabled Mwasimba to focus on growing the business, and in turn provide for the family financially.

Mwasimba, a self-made billionaire had ventured into business at the age of fifteen. He had made his seed money after he convinced his father to let him sell part of their farm produce to traders in their hometown.

After a few transactions of selling potatoes, bananas, and avocados, Mwasimba refunded the cost price plus some profit to his father but kept the extra money he made from quoting a price higher than what his father had indicated. He later registered a business.

Over time the company grew from a one-man enterprise into its current status of a multinational group of companies, employing thousands of people in real estate, manufacturing, investments in information technology and agriculture.

As the Mwasimba children grew older, with the youngest reaching his teens, Patience started to tend to the home library, and took charge of filing the company's confidential documents. She later became one of the directors of the company.

Now, Patience had one wish, to one day have grandchildren to visit or reside with her. Space was not an issue in the Mwasimba family residence within the Karen suburbs of Nairobi. The home, hidden from the outside world by mature trees in the five-acre compound had more than enough space for her family of five sons.

The house which compared to few others in the city had nine bedrooms, most of them with attached bathrooms.

When all the children lived at home, there were three extra bedrooms – two for visitors and one for a nanny on occasions when she was needed to sleep in the main house. There was also a three-bedroom house for domestic workers, located within the expansive compound.

On the few occasions when Richie had mentioned that he and Sophia planned to move out to a separate residence, the response from Patience was simple, "What would be the difference? The north wing is almost a house on its own, only connected to the main house by the family room."

Patience had asked why Richie and Sophia were planning to move out so fast after marriage. Her other sons, Michael and Bill had lived in the same north wing with their wives for at least two years after marriage. She wished Richie and Sophia would stay for even just one year.

Towering above Sophia by two inches, Patience said, "You must be tired after a long day of work at the office. You may go rest while we finish cooking."

"I would like to stay, unless I am getting in the way," Sophia said as she scanned the large kitchen, its uniformity broken by the six-pot cooker, a massive fridge, a single sink near the cooker and a double one at the far end of the room, near the kitchen windows. "I completed all my job tasks for the day, nothing else to do until Richie arrives." She explained as she moved closer to Patience while she inhaled the appetizing aroma from the food on the cooker.

Sophia observed as Patience stirred broccoli soup on the cooker. Since her marriage, she had spent time in the kitchen with Patience, helping with minor tasks. At other times, she simply stood and watched as Patience prepared food.

Patience had given up trying to discourage Sophia from performing household tasks, unaware that Sophia had her own plan, she needed to learn from Patience, not only how to manage the six regular workers in the compound, but also how to prepare food that Richie liked to eat. That way, when they moved to their house, she would have a good idea how to manage her household. She was also aware that Richie had close to zero skills in food preparation, and she looked forward to cooking a balanced diet for her husband.

Patience let the soup simmer while she brought a tray with plates, "Come, let's go," she invited Sophia to follow her. She placed the tray on the six-seater dining table in the smaller of the two dining rooms as Theresa came in to set the table.

Patience and Sophia walked further on and sat in the larger dining room. A short while later the door into the living room opened and Richie stepped inside the house.

Sophia stood up, walked towards Richie and returned his kiss. "Welcome home. How was your day?" She asked as she took the laptop bag off his left shoulder.

"Very productive," he said as he encircled a hand on Sophia's waist, and waved a greeting to his mother as they walked towards the north wing.

Sophia held Richie's arm. "You look tired. How did your evening go?" She asked as she opened the door to their bedroom.

"I am surprised that I look tired, I got a lot of energy in the afternoon, and even completed the PowerPoint presentation. Tomorrow I will get feedback from Mike before I can call it a final copy."

"Are you aware he will be away at a meeting in the morning?"

"Our appointment is not until the afternoon," Richie said as he cupped her face in his hands and kissed her. She tickled him on the stomach. He made to chase her but changed his mind.

She took long strides and sat on the dresser chair. "I will wait and walk out with you to eat dinner." She watched Richie as he removed his coat and stepped out of his trousers. He loosened his necktie as he walked to the bathroom.

She could tell he was tired or worried, so she tried to cheer him up. "Pick the shortest song for today's shower, not your usual fifty-minute one."

"I will be faster if you come scratch my back."

"That will result in a lot of delay."

Sophia was surprised when Richie appeared from the bathroom in less than twenty minutes. "Was the water too hot or too cold for you?"

"The food, that aroma followed me into the bathroom." He extended a hand to her. "Let's go."

When she stood, he embraced her for a long moment until she struggled to free from his tight grip. "I thought you wanted to go eat?"

He loosened his grip before she stood on her toes, reached his mouth, and kissed him. "Welcome back to where you belong."

They walked out of the bedroom while holding hands. The lovebirds sat in the family room of the north wing, chatting, and playing cards until Patience appeared. "Dinner is served, and your father is not joining us tonight, maybe later for tea."

Richie stretched both hands above his head and yawned. "I would have skipped dinner for sleep if not for that nice aroma following me everywhere."

Sophia stood up and extended a hand to Richie. He stretched both arms towards her but heaved himself up without touching her hands.

Patience walked ahead, and the two followed her to the dining room. Patience sat at the far end, Sophia on her left, while Richie sat across, opposite Sophia.

"I will pray, to thank whoever cooked," Richie said as he bowed his head and said grace.

When they said amen, Sophia stood up, picked a bowl next to Richie and served broccoli soup. She placed the bowl on the flat plate right in front of him. She did the same for Patience, and then served herself.

A moment later, Richie mumbled, "I have waited for this all my life."

Sophia looked up from her bowl of soup. "Mum cooked the soup. Look up so she can hear your compliment."

"You got me wrong. I meant, waiting to be served."

Sophia and Patience laughed.

Sophia's lips parted, like she wanted to say something. Instead, she scooped soup into her mouth to distract herself from voicing words that almost escaped from her mouth. She had wanted to tell Richie that she would serve him more often once they moved to their house.

She silently rebuked herself for almost breaking the promise she had made earlier in the day. She turned in the direction of Patience. "I totally agree with Richie. The soup is delicious. Next time, I will learn how to cook it, A to Z."

"Do you have time to toil both in the office and at home in the kitchen?" Richie asked as he softly stepped on her toes under the table.

She stared at him, picked his plate, stood, and served him the main meal of mashed potatoes, beef stew and green vegetables.

Patience held onto her plate as Sophia's hand went for it. Patience shook her head. "Thanks. I will serve myself after I finish my soup."

Sophia served food on her plate and sat down to eat.

Richie stared at Sophia as he addressed Patience. "Mum why are you competing with me?"

Patience chuckled. "Why do you complain when my daughter volunteers to serve me?"

Sophia laughed, followed by silence as Patience served food.

As soon as they finished eating, Richie stood up. "Thanks for dinner. I must retire to bed now. Good night, Mum." He winked at Sophia and walked away.

"No dessert or tea for you?" Patience raised her voice for Richie to hear.

Sophia spoke in a lowered voice. "He needs an early rest as he's been tackling a complicated assignment at work."

"Finally, he has been faced with an issue he had to struggle to solve," Patience chuckled. "His childhood nickname was nutcracker for there were very few problems he could not solve." She stood and walked into the kitchen and back carrying a tray with a tea flask, cups, sugar, and spoons.

Sophia looked at the tray. "Thanks Mum. No tea for me today. I will keep you company while you enjoy your cup of tea."

Patience looked at the clock on the wall showing 9:05pm before she picked up the flask and served tea into her cup. "Does hot chocolate work for you, or some wine?"

"Chocolate, though not tonight. For wine, you will have to train me, starting with my very first sip."

Patience sipped from her cup of tea before placing it on the saucer. "Where have you been hiding the serving skills?"

Sophia looked at her with widened eyes. Patience read the questioning facial expression and explained, "I could tell that Richie liked his food more because you served him." She lifted the cup of tea closer to her mouth but did not sip. "Do not get me wrong, I am not asking that you do it. I just noticed how well he ate after you served him."

Sophia laughed loudly, and then placed a hand on her mouth to quieten herself. "Until I left home, I never saw Papa serve food on his plate. Mama always did it, so I assumed."

"That was cute, though I rarely see you do it. You may do that more often if it does not bother you."

"I would love to, but I feel shy when Dad or the other family members are around."

"Oh, my daughter, I know you are just starting. You will soon realize that in marriage it is the small words and deeds that make the biggest difference."

She lifted her cup and sipped while looking at Sophia with smiley eyes. "Do it if that is your way, and more importantly, if you and your husband are happy with it."

A sparkle appeared in Sophia's eyes as she looked at the clock. "Thanks Mum. I will remember that. Hope Dad will not mind."

"I doubt. What we have always encouraged our children to do from an early age is to be themselves, each one different. You are now family, so be different."

"Thanks," Sophia said as she blinked back tears welling up her eyes. "I see the hands of the clock are rushing. I will go to bed. We have an early morning meeting."

"Going with Richie?"

"We have an official meeting at Two Hills. I will be there with Michael. Good night Mum. See you tomorrow." Sophia walked out of the dining room.

Patience stared at her until she turned right, into the corridor to the north wing.

"I wish I had known you were behind me," Richie called out from the bathroom where he was brushing teeth.

"What would you have done differently, my dear?"

"I would have waited for you to add toothpaste to my brush. Come. I will do that for you."

"No way will I skip that," Sophia said as she entered the bathroom.

Richie stood upright from his bent position by the sink. "You have so far made me an incredibly happy man. I have a strong feeling there is more happiness on the way," he said as he gave her the toothbrush.

Chapter 6

Rules are there to be broken." Richie exclaimed as he entered Sophia's office.

She turned her eyes to the clock on the wall and back to him. "How was your presentation? From the look on your face, you must have had fun," she said as she lifted her hand to meet Richie's for a high-five.

"There is no way one can have fun when their objective is to convince those company directors, and—"

The connecting door opened, and Michael walked in. "Hi. You did an excellent job, Richie. You're among the few people who can manage George with his many questions on figures and volatility of international markets."

"Thanks," Richie said as he moved two steps away from Sophia's desk. "Those directors fractured my soul. The reason I am here for mending." He winked at Sophia, as his round eyes brightened into a smile. He adjusted his necktie, like it wasn't holding the collar of his white shirt well.

Michael cleared his throat to get Richie's attention. "The best part is that today is Friday," he said, as he raised his wrist and glanced at his Rolex. "And the time is 4:50pm."

Both men laughed as they shook hands and continued to talk about the proposed department. Sophia focused on her computer screen.

A short while later, Michael walked closer to Sophia's desk and tapped, like he was knocking on a door. She made eye contact as he said, "Have a nice evening. Sunday tea will be at mine if parents do not insist on a family meal at the club," he said as he walked towards the connecting door.

Richie's eyes followed Michael. "Who drinks tea? I will come only if there will be beer."

Michael gave a thumbs-up as he stepped into his office and the door closed behind him.

"I will drive my wife home if she's not working late on a Friday evening," Richie said to Sophia.

Sophia shut down her computer, pulled her handbag out of a drawer and stood up. "I am out of here. Turn the knob to lock the door when you leave."

By the time she reached the front side of her desk, Richie had walked to the door and opened it. He leaned against the door jamb with hands crossed on his chest, and legs at the ankle and stared as she arrived at the door. "After you, please," he motioned her to walk ahead.

She extended her pointer finger and raised his chin upwards. "This is an office, not a place to feel loving," she admonished while laughing.

Richie removed his coat and held it with two fingers behind his left shoulder. He caught up with Sophia near the elevator.

She stared as he approached. "You have broken our agreement on office behaviour, two times in one week."

He grabbed her waist with both hands, bent and whispered warm air into her ear. "You need to visit Truphena Towers and get to see that even Chairman celebrates whenever he nears a breakthrough."

He freed her as a project officer in his department approached the elevator. "Hello," he looked from Sophia to Richie. "I see you are ready for the weekend."

They returned the greeting. Richie held Sophia's hand while chatting with the man. The elevator stopped on the 5th floor and the man walked out. "Bye. Have a nice weekend," he waved as the elevator doors closed them inside.

Richie squeezed Sophia's hand. He was happy, delighted with his performance at the board meeting, though he would not bring himself to share the details with Sophia. The questions thrown at him had been tough, but he answered to the satisfaction of the company directors. He was almost sure that he would soon have more work responsibilities, even a promotion.

As the elevator neared the parking garage, Sophia tilted her head upwards and made eye contact. He lowered his head, met hers as the elevator chimed and the two doors parted. He was happy, almost certain that his plan to invite her out for dinner and talk her into resigning from her job would succeed.

~~~~~~

At six o'clock Richie parked the Volvo in the driveway, near the entrance to the house. "This car must be tired. I will go bring out the one we are using tonight."

Richie was fond of cars, especially the latest models of sports cars. So, there was no way he would drive the Volvo for their evening out.

His friends referred to him as the man of designer suits and sports cars. Even after marrying and deciding he would spend most of his free time with Sophia, he still made time to visit showrooms, to test-drive the latest arrivals.

She abruptly turned her head, and their eyes met. "I had no idea we were going out tonight. You are full of surprises."

He winked at her as he smoothed his hand down her arm. "Love takes people places. No need for appointments between us, especially on a Friday."

She pushed her tongue out near his face. "Wait until one day I tell you love has asked we visit my village." She let herself out of the car as Richie said, "We can commandeer the helicopter there tomorrow. Our grand arrival will make your grandmother the happiest person in the village."

Sophia let herself into the house through the main door. She peeked into the kitchen and greeted Patience, "Good evening Mum. How was your day?" before she
~~~~~~

headed for the north wing. A few minutes later, she returned to the kitchen. "Mum, are any of your chocolate cakes available? I need to chew on something sweet."

Patience covered the food she was stirring and walked to the dining room. "I have tea ready for everyone. Come."

Theresa followed them, pushing a kitchen trolley, and set the table for tea - five cups, teaspoons, a tea kettle, sugar, side plates, mandazi donuts, and a half-moon chocolate cake.

Richie entered the dining room as Sophia served a piece of the cake into a side plate. He cleared his throat to get her attention. "Spoiling your appetite before our dinner?" He asked, with his hand on Patience's shoulder, as she said a prayer before tea.

"Tea has always been a good appetizer," Sophia said. "You might find some cake if you join us soon." She bit a large chunk of the cake as he watched.

Patience poured tea into her cup while she looked at Sophia from the corner of her eye. She picked a mandazi as she asked, "How is the cake?"

"I might finish all of it. Tastes like the food I needed," Sophia said as Richie pulled up a chair and sat beside her. She served tea into two cups, placing one in front of him as she asked, "Mandazi, or do you plan to fight with me for the cake?"

"I will do with two mandazi, please."

Sophia served three mandazi into a side plate and handed it to Richie, aware that Patience was watching her.

She served a second piece of cake onto her plate. "Cake is filled with sugar only when mass-produced for grocery stores. Mum baked this one with just the right amount of ingredients."

Richie elbowed her arm, softly. "Just enjoy your cake. We can hit the gym tomorrow," he said as he lifted his cup of and took a sip of tea.

"No luck about the gym. I promised myself a lot of sleep in the morning before my friend arrives in the afternoon. Patty will come over for girl talk," Sophia explained as she glanced from Patience to Richie.

Richie picked a mandazi. "Sounds like a busy weekend. Remember, Sunday evening tea will be at Mike's house."

Patience looked up from her plate at the mention of Michael. "Is he aware that Beauta will be here for tea? No worries, I will reconfirm with them again." She said, as she refilled her cup while looking at Sophia who was serving a third piece of cake.

Chapter 7

Sophia and Richie left the north wing at seven-thirty. She was dressed in a light hazel DVF wrap dress and three-inch cream pumps.

He wore casual almond-brown trousers decorated with a fake line of cell phone case pockets from waist to ankle. A light brown turtleneck shirt, and carried a matching zip-down wool sweater, to counter the cold June temperatures.

They stopped by the dining room where they chatted briefly with Mwasimba, Patience and Nick, Richie's younger brother before walking out to the Jaguar parked near the entrance into the house.

Richie held the passenger door open for her. As she prepared to lower herself into the seat, he held her by the shoulders, took one step back and inspected her from head to waist.

"I know I have said this many times before but allow me to say it again. You look lovely each day." He planted tender bites on her lips.

She pulled away from him and stretched her neck towards the house. "Don't forget Dad is in there."

He tickled her neck. "He's busy, chatting with his wife and their baby."

She poked him on the arm.

He returned the gesture by nestling her on the neck. "I am a lucky man," he said as he helped her into the seat.

Sophia pulled Richie's hand to her lips. "Thank you. You too are stunning. I am blessed to have you as my forever." She chuckled. "And you crowned it by complimenting my colours tonight."

He closed the door slowly, like he was afraid it would go beyond the hinge and hit her, walked around to the driver's seat and the engine roared.

The night guards, one on either side of the gate saluted as the metallic grey car accelerated out.

There was silence as Richie drove down the private road to join the main road.

Seeing that Richie was focused on the road, she retrieved her cell phone from her brown Bea Valdes and called Stella, her mother. "Good evening Mama. How's everyone at home?"

"Very fine," her mother answered in a high volume.

Sophia asked her how her younger brothers were faring with their schoolwork. From the positive responses she received, Sophia could tell that her mother and people at home were happy and fine.

She called Joy, her immediate follower. After a short chat, she disconnected and called Silas, Joy's follower.

After about seven minutes of telephone calls, Sophia put the phone back into her bag and looked in Richie's direction. "Those kids sound very unhappy each time we talk. Do you think they will ever learn to proceed with their lives without me by their side?"

Richie down the car as he broke into loud laughter before he said, "Please make arrangements we visit them soon. In the meantime, do me a favour please."

Sophia tilted her head sideways for a better view of Richie as he elaborated on his plea. "Before we visit Joy and Silas, you will need to explain to them how happy you and I are together." He placed his left hand on her thigh. "That way, they will learn to find their own happiness."

"You make it sound so easy, did you ever miss your brothers when they moved out of home to university, or to their houses with their wives?"

"Never. Maybe. But I always knew they were fine, enjoying their lives." He cleared his throat. "That way, I managed to move on with my life," he said as he commandeered the car to a parking at the Devonshire Country Club.

Sophia forced a smile. How she missed her parents and siblings, though it was barely two months ago when they had all been happy at her wedding. She had since visited Joy and Silas twice, and they had visited her once, but she still missed them.

Richie switched off the engine and turned to Sophia.

She opened her Bea Valdes and fumbled for something inside. Her action was to distract Richie from seeing the mist in her eyes. She was teary on recalling how far she had come with her sister Joy.

Sophia and Joy had lived in a one-room house, long before they moved to the apartment now shared by Joy and Silas, their third residence in the city.

The single room was in Kawangware, a crowded low-income residential area in Nairobi. They had only vacated the room after a daytime robbery. One evening they arrived home and found most of their household items gone, including a bale of second-hand clothes that they traded in as their main source of income.

She spoke, to distract Richie from noticing the tears threatening to drop out of her eyes. "I had no idea we were coming here."

Richie, already out of the car, re-entered and placed a hand on Sophia's shoulder. "Did you have a different place in mind? Please name it, and we will be out of here."

"You always forget to ask me for my opinion." She sniffed back the tears. "We did not discuss our destination." She said, though the idea in her mind was different, vivid images of their last visit to that club, the ladies who had hugged and smooched Richie and asked who Sophia was.

Shifting his hand from her shoulder to her face, he said, "Trust me. No. I know you already do. What I meant to say is trust that we will have fun at this place." He stepped out of the car, walked around, and opened her door. As she stepped out, he encircled her waist with both hands and nuzzled her.

She struggled to free herself, "Our feet will get stuck, and we'll become statues for the club."

He tightened his grip on her waist. "That will be my moment, being with you permanently, for future generations to see how much we love one another."

He kissed her and loosened his grip. "I remembered we should not become statues before we make our own children, the ones that will become future generations." He held her hand, and they walked towards the entrance to the club.

"You scare me when you mention children so soon. We still have time."

He paused and looked at her. "We have all the time, but do we have to wait for the time to pass?

She snapped. "I have one request to make."

Richie's eyebrows rose towards his forehead as his round eyes opened wider. Sophia continued. "That you drop that implied topic, together with the beam on your face. That way I will be able to enjoy our evening, our weekend and everything else." She threw both hands up in the air, in resignation.

The mention of children had reminded her of an idea she had not implemented. She had pending plans to visit Justine, her best friend from university. Justine was married and already had two children. Sophia was to ask her about the safest pregnancy barrier for women her age after she'd heard that some could bar one from ever becoming pregnant.

Having been a virgin until her wedding night, Sophia had never taken interest in educating herself on family planning methods, as many of the single women at university did.

Richie's mention of children had reminded her that she had been so busy with her PA duties, she had not made time to meet with Justine.

Richie regretted his words about children on seeing the sudden irritation they brought to his wife. He stopped by the main door to the club, cuddled and kissed her and only stopped after she returned his kiss, a sign that she was back to her usual jovial mood.

They entered the club through the bar. As they stepped inside, the smile on Sophia's face disappeared, while Richie's widened.

A welcome song started from one table, followed by whistling from another table. Before the couple could fully comprehend what was happening, the bar broke into song and handclapping. *"Yee tumeingia, tumeingia. Yo yo, tumeingia yoyo, tumeingia."* (We've arrived, we've arrived. Here we come, here we are.)

Richie tightened his hold on Sophia's waist when he felt her body tense up. He pulled her closer as she tightened her grip on his left arm. He waved back to the patrons in the bar as they repeated the song with words supposedly from Richie and Sophia announcing their arrival, "tumeingia."

Sophia forced a smile, convincing herself that the patrons were happy to see them back at the club as a newly married couple. She waved back to the crowd and was relieved when the clapping and whistling subsided. She whispered to Richie, "I wish you had alerted me."

"I had no idea this would happen. Remember, we have been at other clubs and nothing like—"

A group of ladies ran their direction, interrupting.

Sophia recognized some of them from her last visit to the club and others from her wedding.

The ladies surrounded and hugged Sophia from all sides. "Welcome back. How is your new life? How is your husband? What is it like to be married? I cannot wait to hear more about your honeymoon and after...," were some of the words Sophia could discern as the ladies all spoke simultaneously.

Sophia returned each hug without answering any of their questions before she held Richie's hand and they walked together around the room, greeting friends and acquaintances.

They found a table with two empty seats where they joined two other couples. Sophia was glad the table sat only six people, which meant questions about her marriage and honeymoon would be few, limited to the two women at the table. The men were already busy talking with Richie about the latest car models in town.

~~~~~~

It was long past midnight when Sophia and Richie left the club to go home. She could not hide her happiness. "Oh, I am very tired, but I enjoyed every minute of our visit to the club." She kissed Richie.
~~~~~~

He unbuckled his seat belt and pulled her face back to his. "Thanks for making me the man of the night at the club. I feel much fulfilled," he said, pressing his right hand on his chest, heart.

Richie reversed the car out of the parking into the driveway and turned off the ignition. "I have no words to explain how proud I am of you, my wife." He cleared his throat to make his voice audible, "You are my dream come true."

Sophia squeezed his arm and lined up her forehead with his, they had complete eye contact. He cuddled her. "I hope no one gave you a difficulty time tonight."

She tickled him on the stomach, a place she knew would get him laughing.

He pulled away. "Allow me to get you home, and then you can tickle me all night." He buckled his seat belt, started the engine and the car sped out of the club.

Silence engulfed the car for about five minutes before Sophia spoke. "At one point, the words you said to me after our trip to Rome—"

She stopped when Richie took a quick glance to her side, and only continued after he turned his eyes back to the road. "The words came back to my mind."

"What words?"

"I remember you struggling to explain that the ladies at the club would change, become better, once we were married. I saw it all tonight." She chuckled before continuing, "Though I am yet to understand how instantaneously human beings transform themselves. The same women, who were mean to us not so long ago, were all smiles tonight, wishing us well. The world is perplexing."

Still focused on the road ahead, Richie juggled ideas in his mind. He pondered if he should tell Sophia that the behaviour of the ladies was one reason he vowed never to marry any girl who was a regular of the clubs. "They are the nagging sisters I never had. We men hear that women nag. When will you give me a taste of that?"

"Praying for a nag? It will be worse for you since you never had sisters to give you preparatory doses over the years."

"Really?"

"The only luck you might have is firstborn children, like me rarely nag, nor do my mother's children."

"Okay. That means I will have to wait until our daughter is born and old enough to nag her parents."

"Nice dream you have. It will come true after five or ten years," she said in a raised voice.

He placed a hand on her thigh and turned his focus to the open gates. He drove into the compound, careful not to run over the family dogs that had rushed towards the car.

Watching through the side mirrors, he saw the dogs turn and walk behind the car. He drove and parked near the entrance to the house, walked round the car and assisted her out and into the house.

He could have let Sophia out and driven to park the car at the garage, where his father preferred all cars parked. However, he did not, aware that Sophia feared the guard dogs, though they no longer barked at her as before. "The car will stay there until tomorrow morning. Not my time of night to drive to the garage," he said as he punched a code to open the front door into the house.

The sensor lights illuminated their way to the north wing.

While in the shower, Richie juggled several ideas in his mind. He was trying to interpret Sophia's reaction and response upon his mention of children. He also wondered how he had let the evening go by without asking her to resign from her job.

He hoped Sophia was not serious when she talked of waiting for five to ten years before having children. If that was the case, she would have no reason to resign from her PA job. He shook his head vigorously to dispel the thought from his head.

He stayed on in the shower long after he had seen Sophia leave the bathtub and go to the bedroom.

Lost in thought, Richie soaped his hair twice. He worried that perhaps there was a problem that she found hard to share with him. What could make a happy Sophia become irritated and annoyed at the mention of children?

Richie reminisced on their wedding. Images of how happy Sophia was at their honeymoon poured into his mind. He smiled as he recalled how they had happily discussed the number of children they planned to have, and they had settled on three or four.

He turned off the tap and left the shower cubicle, dressed, and went into the bedroom. He paused in his step, wondering if he should wake her up to discuss the issues that were troubling him, and her.

"Are you asleep or awake for our nightly prayer, Sophia?" He was glad when she did not respond. He switched off his bedside lamp, thoughtful. He would wait for her to mention the topic of starting a family.

Sophia lifted her head from the pillow, startling Richie from his thoughts, she snuggled on his chest.

Chapter 8

Sophia hurried through her afternoon tasks. She packed all the paperwork for the trip to Rwanda before walking out of her office.

Justine had been waiting for ten minutes. They had agreed to meet for tea at 4:30pm, at their favourite eatery in the city. It was now 4:40pm.

Justine was to leave at 5:30pm with her husband. Otherwise, she would have to use public transport which would take her more than an hour to get home, for a journey that usually takes twenty-five minutes to drive.

Sophia entered the restaurant and saw Justine, hard to miss with her above average height of six-foot one, and mauve-coloured hair. Sophia increased her stride towards the corner table where Justine sat. "I am so sorry," she opened her arms wide and embraced her. "I have missed you. This married life and work have come between our friendships."

Justine patted Sophia on the shoulder. "Welcome into the club, sometimes it offers the best life, other times not." She laughed loudly, but never appeared to mind that heads had turned their direction. "That sounds like there is a balance, not too good, not too bad," she added.

A waiter walked to their table and greeted Sophia. Many of the staff at the eatery were familiar with the two women from their after-work visits to the place, especially before Sophia's wedding.

"A hot cup of tea for me," Sophia said before she lowered her eyes and pointed to the cake in front of Justine, "And a similar cake."

Justine waited until the waiter was out of earshot. "Why did I think you had sworn off cake, and other sugary foods?"

"I will eat and blame you after, for enticing me into that type of sugar," She said while pointing at Justine's cake.

The two friends stayed quiet as the waiter placed Sophia's order in front of her, wished them a nice evening and walked away.

Justine lifted her cup close to her mouth and held it there. "So, how is the life of living with a man every day?" She lowered the cup, "At the office and at home? The last time we met you decided to be shy, not to talk."

"I have not changed"

Justine took a sip from her cup, placed it on the table and leaned forward, more towards Sophia, seated opposite from her. "I am married. I live with a man. How is your life living with in-laws?"

"Better than all the stories along these streets," Sophia said, waving a hand towards the outside of the restaurant. "So far, I like residing there, but we plan to move out soon."

"Is it that you do not want to make babies from your in-laws' house?"

Sophia broke the eye contact and took a bite of her cake. "I know you long for me to join you soon. Two kids already…, will I ever catch up?"

"Why not? Get your babies one year after the other or pray for twins."

Justine watched as the glint faded from her friend's face. She extended a hand and touched Sophia's arm. "Why do you look so scared? No need to fear the word twins, or even triplets, when your husband can pay people to serve you in bed."

Sophia scanned her surrounding, then turned back to Justine. "It is not about twins. I want to work for some years before we start a family, babies." She chuckled. "I know you have done enough research. Which family planning would you recommend?"

"Which family do you want to plan?" Justine immediately regretted her words, so she clarified. "I meant to say, sometimes it is better to get children while still young, especially if you and your husband can afford to"

"We agreed about children, but not when."

Sophia was surprised when Justine extended both hands, smoothed Sophia's cheeks and whispered, "You live with your husband. You will need to go for a pregnancy test before you talk of barriers." She chuckled. "I will buy you tea every day for one year if you are without a baby yet. Look at your smooth and glowing skin."

She watched as Sophia's hand lifted to her cheeks. "You are not being helpful. That is not what I came to discuss."

Justine sipped from her cup, checked her watch, and sipped more tea. She could tell Sophia was thoughtful, reflecting on what she had told her about her assessment and prediction. Justine decided it was better to distract her, remove the worry on her face. "I remember the talk I received before my wedding."

She saw Sophia's face brighten up, so she added, "The nonsense some of my aunts were happy to dispense, how not to get pregnant at my honeymoon." She chuckled. "I forgot everything, being busy with the wedding. Their words came to haunt me soon."

Sophia's eyebrow rose, in question. "What?"

"Their advice resonated with me after our honeymoon when we realized our first-born baby was on the way."

Sophia lifted her cup of tea nearer to her mouth. "How is your life at work with two babies at home?" She took a sip, replaced the cup on the table and forked the last piece of cake into her mouth.

Justine was aware Sophia wanted to change the topic, from herself to something else, so she said, "Work is good, though I am looking at other places with more pay. Sometimes I feel like all I do is work, earn to pay the nanny and feed the family."

"But you have a good nanny who's stayed with you since baby number one. Is that not so?"

"I do not have any complaints in that department, especially when I hear stories of what some of the women go through. Some will be in the office one day and not show up the next. They will call and say they have an emergency, no nanny to leave their children with. I am lucky with mine."

Justine checked her watch again. "If I were you, I would not move out of my in-laws' house, especially if baby number one is on the way." She winked at Sophia. "There is nothing more comforting than leaving for work each morning, knowing your baby is with someone you trust, a person who truly cares about the baby."

"Wooi, Justine. Why are you talking so much about babies, or are you already with baby number three?"

"After you please," Justine touched Sophia's arm. "You need to hurry up. That way, I can start on my baby number three, and maybe leave the employment world for a while."

Sophia sneered. "Stop working?"

"When we start on our third baby, I will tell my husband to do all the money-earning work while I stay home to regain my sanity, and energy." She smiled. "I will take a long leave or find a better job." She pushed her chair back and stood up. "I will rely on you to find me a well-paying job at your company."

Sophia followed suit, stood up. "Time has passed so quickly." She picked up the bill, walked to the cashier and paid.

They left the eatery and walked to Akoth Towers where Justine was to meet with her husband. At the entrance to the building, Sophia hugged Justine. "Thanks for coming for tea with me. Make more plans. We'll go for another after I come back from Rwanda."

Justine returned the hug. "Next tea will be at my house. You need to come and see for yourself how nice it is to have kids running all over the house."

Sophia fisted her hand and pushed Justine's shoulder, gently. "You are too much about babies. Go make another one with your husband. There he comes," she pointed to the car which just stopped at the drop-off point. They moved closer to the car where she greeted Justine's husband and bid them goodbye.

Sophia walked into Akoth Towers, more worried than when she had left her office. Her hope had been that Justine would tell her something different, other than the possibility that she could be pregnant.

Chapter 9

She stepped out of the car and wiped her forehead with the back of her hand. It would take long for anyone to convince Sophia that she was not sweating.

Feeling warm in July was a contradiction, July being the coldest month of the year when maximum temperatures dropped as low as fifteen degrees Celsius. A month when many people in the city could be seen clad in warm sweaters and jackets.

She felt tired as she picked her handbag, blaming her early morning fatigue on hunger. She had woken up late and had no time left to eat breakfast.

Sophia was surprised and glad to see Janet from the company travel office. Since her engagement to Richie, the farthest place Janet had helped her was at the check-in desk.

Janet or another staff from the company travel office was always at the airport, whenever a company director or a member of the Mwasimba family was traveling.

Being Richie's wife meant she was now part of the Mwasimba family, the reason she was being received on arrival.

She forced the best smile she could in her state of tiredness. "Good morning Janet. Am I late for the flight?"

Janet laughed while pushing the airport trolley with Sophia's two bags. One had her personal items and the other a laptop and official documents for Michael's two-day meeting in Kigali, Rwanda.

"You have enough time to check-in and relax. Michael insisted to wait for you so that you check in together."

Sophia saw Michael as they walked towards the premier check-in desk. At a height of six-foot three, and with the confidence of a company director, he was easy to pick out from a crowd. He stared as Sophia and Janet walked towards the check-in desk.

Janet handed their travel documents to the check-in clerk, and within minutes the trio were on the escalator going upstairs.

Sophia almost voiced her gratitude when Janet turned the direction of the airport executive lounge. She was glad for the chance to eat breakfast at the lounge.

While Michael was still studying the menu, Sophia looked at the waiter. "I will have the full breakfast," she pointed to the third item on the menu.

Michael closed the menu and tossed it on the table. "I will have the same." He turned to Sophia, "Could be our only meal until after our afternoon meeting."

"I pray you are not right," Sophia said and immediately regretted her words. Since there was no way to retract them, she looked at Michael and smiled.

He noticed her uneasiness and said, "You are right. Kigali is a stone throw away. There will be enough time to eat lunch before the meeting."

As they ate, Sophia reflected on the sleep that had robbed her of time to eat breakfast, which was on the dining table as she left the house. She also recalled the sad look on Richie's face when she hardly paused at the dining table. Instead of sitting down to eat, she had filled a glass with juice and gulped it in one go.

Her action had compelled Richie to stand up. He had placed his napkin on the table, kissed her on the cheek and wished her journey mercies before he marched out of the house.

Michael interrupted Sophia's internal reflections as he talked about their business in Kigali and the people they would be meeting.

He also talked about a holiday he and Beauta once made to Kivu Beach in Rwanda. He planned to travel back for another holiday.

Michael wheeled the office bag as they walked into the plane.

Sophia wondered if she should ask for the bag, which had been her responsibility in all their past travels.

She stopped and opened her handbag to check the boarding pass for her seat number.

Michael stopped on realizing she was not by his side. On seeing his action, she increased her stride.

As the air hostess walked ahead to show them to their seats, a worry crept into Sophia's mind, what to do if she was in a seat next to Michael?

She exhaled when she saw her window seat on the opposite side from Michael's aisle seat. She sat and stared as the air hostess placed the office bag in the overhead compartment near Michael before she busied herself looking outside.

The next time Sophia looked in the direction of Michael, he was busy working on his laptop. She retrieved a book from her handbag and proceeded to stay updated on events in finance and marketing.

~~~~~~~

Richie parked his car in the basement of Akoth Towers, walked into the elevator and stood in one corner. Instead of pressing 52nd floor as usual, he pressed ground floor from where he walked outside and turned left to an adjacent building.

He entered a banking hall, cleared through bank security, and walked into Enock's office.

Enock, Richie's childhood friend worked as the manager at one of his father's banking businesses. Their friendship had lasted since their years in kindergarten, so Enock was not surprised when Richie knocked and entered his office that morning. He welcomed Richie,
~~~~~~~

informing him he had a meeting scheduled for nine o'clock that morning - in less than thirty minutes.

Richie and Enock were age-mates, had grown up together, attended the same schools, and frequented similar clubs in the city.

Secondary school separated them when Enock attended a British private boarding school, two hundred kilometers out of Nairobi, from where he proceeded to the UK for his university education. They maintained their friendship through correspondence and get-togethers whenever possible.

Enock and Richie engaged in general discussions until it was five minutes to nine when Enock stood up and Richie followed.

Richie lowered his neck a bit to make proper eye contact with Enock. "I have an issue on which I would like your opinion."

Enock tilted his head upwards for a better view of Richie who was still talking. "I know you are not married, but I need ideas on how to convince my wife to stop working … to resign from her PA position."

"Have you talked with her about it?"

Richie, usually with squared shoulders, looked different, with hunched shoulders. "I have tried, but she likes her PA job too much. She travels a lot. This morning she left for the airport, and I lost it. Can you give her a non-travel job at the bank?"

Richie stopped talking on realizing that he had already shared too much information on the issue troubling him.

Enock held the handle of his office door and looked up at Richie. "Talk with her, let me know what position she would like here. Let's meet next week and discuss when she can start."

Richie extended a hand to Enock. "I am indebted to you. Let me know how to pay back a good friend like you."

"I doubt if you can pay back. The need I have is for a good girl, one I can convince to marry me."

He elbowed Enock's arm gently. "I know a few potentials."

Enock's face lit up into a smile. "The sooner you get back to me, the better," he said as he opened the door and led the way out.

Richie entered Akoth Towers, returned a greeting from the guard at the entrance and walked on. He nodded to the two women behind the reception desk, as his mind wandered to the ambivalence of the waiting lounge marked by subtle crisscrossing white lights. He was in search of something to calm his racing mind.

He paused and surveyed the waiting lounge, where there were two people engaged in a discussion. He walked towards the elevators.

Richie was deep in thought, barely turning his head as he returned greetings from fellow riders. He thought of Sophia on a flight to Rwanda, leaving him home alone.

He relaxed on remembering that his situation was not that bad, he would be with his mother in the evening. He would not have known what to do if he and Sophia had already moved to their own residence, then Sophia traveled and left him alone, with their house staff.

Three weeks earlier, Richie had turned down a work assignment to Europe, letting a different manager travel. He had thought of how lonely he would feel, leaving Sophia behind just a month into their marriage. He had not shared his thoughts with anyone, opting to use the excuse of the research he was involved in for the proposed department. So, he was more than surprised when Sophia chose to travel to Rwanda.

That morning, while waiting for Sophia to join him at the breakfast table, he had been juggling words in his head, wondering how to ask her when she planned to resign from her post. At some point he had hoped that by asking her, she would get upset and make a complaint to Michael. Richie assumed that if she mentioned to him the idea of resigning, Michael would encourage her along, considering that his wife found no need for employment.

Richie had already confirmed with his banking manager that he had enough money to support him and Sophia. She was not a big spender, almost qualifying as frugal, so they would manage a comfortable life on his salary as a manager.

Further, if his income was not enough, he was free to dip a hand into his inheritance, a hefty sum of millions which he had received from his father on his twenty-second birthday, just like his older brothers had received.

Richie was certain it would be okay to use his inheritance, recalling that James, the second-born brother had converted his inheritance into dollars and left for America. He had not been back home since.

There was also some money available for Sophia's use. Before their wedding, Sophia's father had turned down dowry for her hand in marriage. Mwasimba had set the money aside, and asked Richie to access the three million whenever Sophia needed money.

He reflected on how comfortable his brothers were financially, yet their wives did not have jobs. Instead, the wives spent their time out shopping at high-end designer stores. Two or three times a year, they traveled to Europe to attend the London, Milan, and Paris Fashion Week.

Chapter 10

Richie spent the morning hours researching and refining background information for the proposed department. In the afternoon, he closed the folders of the new project and opened his regular tasks as a manager.

He was surprised when Patty entered his office and alerted him of the time. "You still need to go home for a change of clothes, even though your dear wife has traveled."

"Do not give me a reason to ask about your pending marriage, after which we can discuss wives and husbands." Richie countered as he logged off and shut down the computer. He gathered papers from his desk and locked them up in a drawer.

Patty took a few strides forward and stood near his desk with one hand perched akimbo on her waist. She remained in that position until he stood up.

He slipped his coat on and buttoned up as he caught up with her to the elevator. "Thank goodness you interrupted me, only hunger would have alerted me to the passing time, which is not easy as I have no appetite." He straightened the collar of his coat and tightened the necktie.

"She just traveled for two nights. Use the time to reflect on how to welcome her back," Patty said.

He chuckled. "There's some sense from my cousin. My dear wife has had mood swings in the last few days, it could be the travel without me," he said, patting his chest.

"Aaah, more men need to hear that," Patty said as the elevator chimed, and the doors opened. She stepped in and Richie followed.

After the elevator doors closed, she tilted her head in his direction. "As I was saying, girls, sisters are important people to have. Five boys and they grow up with zero knowledge of women, months, mood swings and whatever you guys call it."

He nodded in agreement, prompting Patty to add, "Don't make me wait for long."

Richie shifted sideways and made eye contact with her as she continued. "I am waiting for your daughter or son to be part of my wedding party."

Patty was surprised at how loud Richie laughed. The elevator came to a halt in the basement, and they walked out towards Patty's car.

"I hear it's women who decide when to have or not have children. Have you asked your friend, now your sister, about her plans?"

She danced on her toes. "Sounds like I have a new task. What am I hearing, that you have not discussed that as a couple?"

Richie moved closer to her and whispered, "We have discussed and agreed on the numbers, but not the when. I will mention the topic after I have the new department in operation."

Her left cheek pushed upwards in a questioning manner. She had grown up with Richie as one of her favourite cousins and was glad that she had connected well with Sophia as a friend.

Patty opened the door to her car and sat in the driver's seat. She rolled the window down, pulled the seatbelt across her chest, as she addressed Richie. "Why is it taking you so long with that pretty smart girl?" She grinned. "It's now your turn to learn how to balance your office work with the needs of your wife."

"That would give me double work. My plan is that she resigns and stays home to make decisions for our family, while I work and provide the finances."

"That sounds like there is a problem at my brother's house."

Richie leaned on the side of the car near the window, stared at Patty and whispered, "Hear me. There's no problem, only benefits of marrying an intelligent girl, a virgin." He cleared his throat. "I wonder if there is another one left in this city, except my cousin here," he said as he poked his pointer finger on her shoulder.

She shoved his head away. "Do not tell me you were that lucky, marrying a virgin?"

"Envious?"

"I now understand your need to learn, ASAP." She chuckled. "I will urge your best man to bring you level-one videos and books." Her words were almost lost in her laughter.

Richie tickled her on the armpit. She giggled as she pushed his hand away and rolled up the window, leaving a small opening. "Give me until next weekend. I will come up with ideas to help you in the bedroom." She started the engine, winked at Richie before she drove off.

Richie walked back towards the elevators and entered the company car waiting, they drove home.

~~~~~~~

Richie sat in the library with his feet on a coffee table. He held a journal awfully close to his face, too close for the eyes to decipher the words. He appeared focused, thoughtful, until Patience opened the door and informed him dinner was ready.

He slowly lowered the journal away from his face. "Who wants to eat? I could sit here all night."

Patience walked towards the door. "Your father is waiting for us at the dining table."

The mention of his father waiting immediately prompted Richie into action. Though Richie and his brothers had learned from an early age to share all sorts of jokes with their mother, and occasionally answer her back, they had developed an unexplained respect, tending towards fear for their father.
~~~~~~~

As the Mwasimba five sons grew older, their father's word remained almost final, except on professional matters where they referenced published documents to counter his opinions. Consequently, the mention of his father not eating because Richie had not arrived at the family table was enough to get him moving.

He pushed his feet into the flip flops he had abandoned besides a bookshelf and strolled out of the library. He hastened his stride as he walked through the main sitting room and the large dining room, to reach the smaller one.

He waved a greeting to his father before he washed hands at a nearby sink.

Mwasimba looked at Richie as he sat down with a thump. "I thought you would go research the financial markets in Kigali, while the others attended their meetings?" He asked while serving food onto his plate.

Richie leaned with both hands on the table. "I am waiting for a word from the directors, or Chairman." His face broke into a grin on using the pet-name for their father, Chairman. "A word on seed funds to start me off."

Mwasimba stared at Richie. "After such an important meeting with the Board, it's advisable to always do a follow-up."

Richie lifted his eyes from the empty plate in front of him and looked at his father who was still speaking. "Michael mentored you well into the company but forgot that part. The Board approved your budget estimates as per your request."

With a beaming face, Richie looked at his mother, as his father added. "What are you up to tomorrow? Come by my office, we need to look at the document again."

"Thanks, Dad. No, let me try that again. Thanks, Chairman, for the good news. I am happy I came over for dinner" Richie said, sending his parents into laughter.

Patience said, "You need to spend more time with your father, especially now that you are married. You will learn more than you could ever get from those books in the library."

Richie served food into his plate. "I need a lot of tips on that. Starting a new life with a brand-new wife and a brand-new department is not easy."

Noticing Richie's face had lost the smile, Patience asked, "Has Sophia said if she would like to stay home while you juggle your office work?"

Mwasimba cleared his throat, placed his fork on the plate and looked at his wife. "I wouldn't mention that topic yet. Remember this one is different, still likes the idea of holding a job." He pointed at Richie. "Better if the suggestion to work or not comes from her, not you."

After dinner, Patience went to the kitchen and returned carrying a tray with a tea flask and cups.

She walked past Richie and Mwasimba, prompting them to stand and follow her. Mwasimba quickened his stride. "We need tea, though it looks like we must follow you to get it." He held the library door open for Patience and Richie.

Richie sat next to his father and talked about the range of activities he planned in the first stages of the new department. He was eager, discussing how and which world markets they would focus on, between the global East and West.

Mwasimba had been the initiator of the idea, a department within the company to monitor global financial markets and identify opportunities and gaps for firms in Africa to focus on. He was keen to give caution and suggestions.

He took a long look at Richie. "Once you do a proper assessment, results could point you to the East. They are always awake hours ahead of us, and in bed as the West wakes up."

Richie straightened his back. "That puts us, Africa, at the center, strategically placed to take advantage of lessons learned from the East, so as to prudently tackle the West as they wake up."

"Slow down young man." Mwasimba raised his left hand to quieten Richie. "It will be hard to stay awake for twenty-four hours, to learn from the East and reap from the West." He paused and lifted a teacup to his mouth.

Richie did not respond. Instead, he picked up his cup, stood and paced one side of the 600-square foot library and office. When he returned, he refilled his cup before he spoke. "I hear you. We can start with the East before we strategize for the West."

When Richie noticed a nod from his father, he continued. "Looks like the only time I will be busy is at the beginning. Once everything is set up, I can have staff either in Asia or here. Mumbai would do once the Mwasimba Towers is completed."

"I had no idea the name of the new building has changed."

Richie looked at his father and raised a hand in a mock salute.

Patience excused herself and left the library.

The two men went ahead with their animated discussions on the proposed department. The topic expanded when Richie opened the computer in the library and checked global financial market reports from New York, which had just opened for the day's business.

It was past midnight when Richie and his father left the library.

As Richie switched off his bedside lamp, he was glad, and his earlier worry about Sophia being away from him had evaporated.

More than ever before, Richie was now sure he would be able to support his family financially. There would be absolutely no need for Sophia to continue in employment.

Chapter 11

Three months after her wedding day, whose events still lingered fondly in her heart, Sophia surprised herself. All the breakfast food escaped without warning from her stomach as she approached the car for her drive to the office.

One look at her messed cream skirt-suit made her retreat into the house. On reaching the dining room where Patience was still eating breakfast, she muttered, "Sorry. I soiled my dress. I will change then proceed to the office," as she hurried off to the north wing.

In the fifteen minutes that it took her to have a change of clothes, Patience called and let Michael know Sophia was unwell, and she would not make it to the office for the day.

When Sophia walked out of the house, she did not find the car to take her to the office. She returned inside the house and asked, "Mum, did the driver go on another errand?"

"I released him. Michael is aware you are unwell," Patience informed Sophia.

"I am fine, I will go to work."

"You just vomited. It cannot be the food, for I ate the same and am still okay. You need to see a doctor. I called and made an appointment."

Sophia walked away. She had many questions in her mind belying the anger displayed on her face, her eyebrows almost touching each other. She silently questioned, "Who is Patience to interfere with my PA job? Who is she to decide for me when to stay home and rest, or that I need to visit a doctor, and already she's made an appointment?"

She entered the bedroom and pushed the door shut behind her, harder than she intended. She promised herself that, once she regained balance from the dizziness that was threatening to overwhelm her, she would be on the phone talking with housing agents. They must urgently vacate the north wing if Patience had decided to become the typical controlling mother-in-law.

Sophia rested her head on a pillow and lifted her feet onto the bed to avoid tripping over, she felt dizzy, and all the items in the bedroom seemed in motion, rotating.

A soft knock on the door, followed by the voice of Theresa, "Sophia, Sophia. How are you feeling?" startled her out of sleep.

There was a moment of silence before Theresa spoke again, "Please get ready, and come eat some lunch before your drive to the hospital."

Theresa, a stout 56-year-old grandmother had worked for the Mwasimba family for eighteen years. She had started as a nanny and was now the senior house staff.

She cleaned bathrooms and windows in the main house, supervised the outsourced staff that came and cleaned carpets and floors every fortnight, and went grocery shopping whenever Patience was not available. The other workers always consulted with her on any matter before they went to Patience.

A quick glance to her watch, and Sophia realized she had been asleep for five hours. A thought in her mind haunted her. "You have no life. After your mother-in-law, now the house worker is on your case, asking you to get up and prepare to visit a doctor." She made a mental note on precisely what to say to Theresa the next time she interfered with her sleep. Without mincing her words, she would ask Theresa to stop interfering with her life, focus on her housework instead.

A different thought crossed her mind. Sophia asked herself why she was in such an awful mood. Why she now viewed Patience as her mother-in-law, rather than the caring mother she had been all along?

What had Theresa done to warranty such unkind thoughts, just by knocking on the bedroom door to alert her of the passing time and invite her to eat a meal? Food was what she wanted right then, as her stomach felt empty.

Lunch did the same thing as breakfast. The food rushed out of Sophia's stomach as she stood to leave the dining table. She held onto the lower part of her stomach, like it was about to fall onto the floor. "What is wrong with my stomach today?" She was now in agreement with Patience on a visit the doctor's clinic.

For a moment, Sophia wondered whether the sickness had affected her mind, or had she just seen Patience make a sign of the cross?

From their three months of living together in one house, Sophia had come to acknowledge that Patience was religious, a strong believer in some higher powers.

Every Sunday the family spent the morning at church and some afternoons at a city kitchen where they served a meal to street children, the family's way of giving back to society.

Sophia questioned why Patience must pray for everything. 'Did she just pray for Sophia to get better, or stop throwing up yucky food all over her house and compound? Or was the prayer over something else? She contemplated as she walked into the bedroom for another change of clothes.

In the bedroom, she sat on the edge of the now well-made bed. Theresa had changed the duvet and sheets within the brief span of time Sophia was away eating lunch.

For a moment, Sophia felt guilty, and asked herself why she harboured negative thoughts towards Patience and Theresa, something which was quite contrary to her upbringing.

Stella, her mother raised her children to respect people, more so those who helped them, just the way Patience, Theresa and the Mwasimba Company had done for her.

The company employed her as a PA and compensated her well enough to pay school fees for her siblings. Otherwise, by now her father would have suffered a heart attack from the stress of buying and selling livestock at a rural market for meagre returns. Heart attacks, the hidden cause of sudden death among many poor people, were rarely ever confirmed in the village, it costs money to do that.

Sophia thought of how comfortable her life was as Richie's wife. She still had her job and lived with caring people.

She picked her phone and informed her husband that she was unwell. Earlier, she had seen his eleven missed calls showing on the screen of her cell phone.

~~~~~~~

Patience sat at the family room of the north wing, thoughtful as she waited for Sophia so that they could set off for the visit to the doctor. She prayed and came to a calm acceptance that in just a short while she would know the truth.

She took solace in the fact that she believed in God and in modern medicine. Whatever the doctor found as the cause of the vomiting, he would provide medication, and she would accept it as God's will.

Patience reflected on how Mwasimba had transferred his greatest fear for the future to her – that there
~~~~~~~

would be no future generations to inherit from his children the business empire he had worked so hard to build.

To Mwasimba, the enterprise was meant to help his grandchildren, rather than his sons. His children had already received their share of his wealth in the form of the best education and healthcare money could buy, and the best food, clothes, and residence. Family holidays, a hefty sum of money on turning twenty-two, and they held senior positions at his Group of Companies.

Patience counselled herself, that as a woman and a mother—"

Sophia strolled into the family room, interrupting Patience's thought process.

Patience stood and followed Sophia outside, to the car, to be driven to the doctor's clinic.

On arrival at the clinic, Sophia wondered if some people in society never arrive late. Dr. Rajur was in his office waiting for her, twenty minutes after 2:00p.m., her appointment time.

The doctor did Sophia a big favour that she promised herself never to forget. He greeted Patience who was walking right behind Sophia into the consulting room, "Nice to have you back after many years. Please stay in the waiting lounge while I consult with the patient."

Patience paused from her walk, "She is my daughter. I could come in—"

The doctor turned to Sophia while addressing Patience. "In future visits," as he ushered Sophia into the consulting room.

Sophia sat on a chair across the table, opposite from that of Dr. Rajur. She stared as he washed hands before he pulled on gloves.

Doctor Rajur appeared to be in his late sixties. He had receding hair, almost reflected by the clear eyeglasses falling from his nose, if not for the string holding them behind his ears.

The white doctor's coat he wore concealed part of his white shirt and red floral necktie. As expected, a stethoscope hung loosely from his neck, on either side of his shoulders, down to his chest.

Sophia answered his many questions, until it felt like she had just bared her whole life story to him. At some interval he stood and examined her tongue, eyes, palms, and fingernails. She guessed he was in search of any signs of her being anemic.

After examining her feet and toenails he discarded the gloves into a nearby garbage bin before he filled in a form then pressed a button on his desk phone.

A nurse knocked on the door and walked into the room.

Dr. Rajur addressed the nurse, "Sophia is feeling dizzy, walk with her to the laboratory. Afterwards, show her to the patient resting room."

The nurse extended a hand to Sophia who held on and stood up. They walked to the lab at one end of the building where Sophia gave urine and blood samples before the nurse guided her into a dayroom, where she could lie down while waiting for the lab results.

Loud noises in the room woke Sophia up. She opened her eyes and saw Dr. Rajur and Richie standing next to her bed, in a conversation.

She considered their chat as intended to wake her up. Otherwise, there would be no reason for them to talk right next to her, asleep.

She struggled to sit up as dizziness pulled her back. She only succeeded when Richie held her hand while supporting her back with his other hand. He kissed her on both cheeks, then on the mouth. "I love you. You will be fine. All is well."

Dr. Rajur looked at her, looked at Richie and back at her. "Young lady, the lab results indicate you are not sick, as you could fear."

Sophia's face brightened with a smile, which disappeared as soon as she heard the doctor complete the sentence. "The Almighty has blessed you. The vomiting is a result of your body adjusting to hold the baby in your womb. I have prescribed medicine for…"

The rest of the words trailed off Sophia's mind. She fell back on the bed into a sleeping position, turned and faced the wall.

Dr. Rajur patted Richie on the shoulder before he left the room.

Richie leaned over and kissed Sophia's wet cheeks. "Thank you for being the carrier of good news, makes us happier as a family."

She did not respond. All he saw were more tears, which left him wondering if the tears were from too much joy, or sadness.

He sat on the edge of the bed, holding her hand, waiting for her to get up for their journey home.

After about ten minutes, there was a soft knock, the door opened, and Patience peered. She glanced from Richie to Sophia and back to Richie.

Richie returned her gaze and waved her away.

Patience obeyed and closed the door behind her.

Richie stayed in the dayroom until Sophia sat up by herself. "When are we going home?"

"Whenever you are ready," he said, as he gently helped her out of the bed. They slowly and quietly walked out of the clinic and boarded the car he had driven to the hospital while Patience left with the driver.

On arrival home, Patience watched as her son and his wife took calculated steps into the house. They stopped at the family room where Patience brought a glass of water which Sophia used to swallow her medicine.

As the couple walked to the north wing, Patience retreated into the kitchen. She needed to start fulfilling what she had waited to do for many years - cook delicious meals for an expectant daughter-in-law.

Chapter 12

The medicines, or perhaps the food, made a remarkable difference. Within the three days of prescribed rest, Sophia regained her energy and promptly resumed work on the fourth day, against the expectations and wishes of both Richie and Patience.

Richie was disappointed. He had hoped that the pregnancy, with its related vomiting and dizziness, would compel Sophia to resign from her job. Stay home to focus on her health and the developing baby in her womb.

With every argument about her going back to work, Sophia reminded Richie that it was time for them to move out of his parents' house, to their own residence. Her reasoning being that they were no longer children, to live with their parents.

At one point, she concluded Richie was not for the idea of changing residence, so she changed her approach. "We can go rent a house while waiting to find your dream home to purchase. Better still, I can go stay with my siblings while you make up your mind. I need complete peace of mind to effectively implement my office duties."

Richie massaged the back of his neck. He scanned the bedroom, like he was searching for someone invisible.

He picked up his cell phone and dialed the housing agent to confirm that he was ready to buy one of the houses he and the agent had liked. Having a happy family was one of his plans as a married man. He was ready to relocate, just to fulfil Sophia's wishes.

The phone on the other end rang twice. While Richie waited for a response, the words his father uttered before his wedding echoed in his mind. "This one is different, still likes the idea of holding a job. Keep that in mind as you negotiate with her."

Richie disconnected the call and turned to Sophia who had been staring at him all that time. He cuddled and kissed her lips. When he released her, she wiped her mouth with the back of her hand, something she had never done before.

It then dawned on Richie that he needed to act fast before a conflict developed between him and his wife.

Alarmed, words escaped from his mouth, "Do you have any preference for an estate to reside at? It will be okay if we find a single-family house. That way there will be no need for us to move again once the babies are born."

Sophia made a swift move of head and made eye contact with Richie. He could tell she was confused when he said babies. He fought back a smile, that Sophia thought she was carrying more than one child.

She shook her head for a no.

Richie, not able to guess if she shook her head because of his mention of babies, or purchase of a single-family residence, chose to remain silent.

Sophia was thoughtful about how she would prefer to live in a nice apartment. Even an apartment at the compound where she left Joy and Silas upon marriage would work for her and Richie.

The location was convenient, near a main road, a shopping mall, and a school. The compound was professionally managed to a high standard of cleanliness and had many pleasant amenities which were rare in many other housing estates in the city.

There was a common room, swimming pool, a park for children to play at, a two-car parking space for each apartment, and visitors' parking.

Sophia recalled that they had neighbours with young children, and the families appeared happy to reside at that estate.

Her thoughts drifted to the passing months and the personalized care she had received from Patience. She doubted whether many mothers-in-law would put themselves at the service of a twenty-five-year-old daughter, the way Patience had done so far. Patience prepared whatever food Sophia wished to eat, and readily provided prayers and words of comfort whenever Sophia voiced any discomfort.

Ever since Sophia's first visit to the doctor, Patience had prepared her breakfast and packed a hot lunch for her to take to work, daily.

On the advice of Patience, Sophia had started to eat a full meal for breakfast. Food combinations normally served for lunch or dinner, and it worked. The vomiting stopped, so did the medication.

Sophia reflected on what it would mean to move to a different residence. No Patience available to prepare her meals, accompany her to doctor appointments, make a sign of the cross to comfort her whenever she was not feeling well, or bring high-end boutique owners into the house, with loads of designer clothes for her growing body.

If Sophia remembered well, which she did, with her trophy for keenness to details - an imaginary trophy from her keen eye regarding her PA tasks - Patience had said many prayers right in front of her, especially whenever eating food had resulted in vomiting.

Sophia was aware that Stella, her mother prayed for her children every morning and every night, at the family prayer sessions. But Sophia could not recall seeing her mother break into a spontaneous prayer whenever one of them was unwell, as Patience unfailingly did for her.

With those thoughts, she concluded that Richie's mother genuinely loved and cared for her. "Can we stay here until after the baby is born?"

The words not only startled Richie but confused him as well. Her message was nothing close to the response he had been anticipating.

It was time for Richie to bite his tongue. If he opened his mouth, chances were high that he might utter the wrong words, words to make Sophia reconsider the pleasant request she had just made.

He cuddled and kissed her on the mouth many times before he stopped and said, "Not good for our baby to run out of oxygen." He was glad she did not wipe her mouth this time round.

Chapter 13

"I have something that will make you happy." Richie said to Sophia on their drive home from work.

Sophia made eye contact with Richie, seated next to her in the backseat. "I am already happy with myself, with you and with life in general." She chuckled. "I would like to hear of the addition to my happiness."

Richie squeezed her hand. "Next week, the office will close for the statutory holiday. I made a booking for us to go on a Safari."

"I wonder how you decided that I would not prefer to stay home and sleep?" she asked in a whisper.

He intertwined their fingers while he mumbled, "More over tea at home."

Richie decided not to tell her more about the Safari, especially his main reason for wanting a pleasant environment - where he would persuade her to resign from her job.

During the rest of the drive home, they discussed the congested traffic in the city, and the amount of time and energy resources wasted in the traffic holdups.

When they arrived home, Sophia changed into a free-flowing yellow floral dress. She added a complimenting metallic belt tied closer to her chest than her waist, and then went to the kitchen to chat with Patience. While there she noticed that Wekesa, the elderly house chef had not stopped stealing quick glances at her. To answer the chef's unvoiced question, she yawned and looked at Patience. "I will leave you and go for a walk. I have been seated most of the day."

"That contradicts what I was about to say, that you pull one of the kitchen chairs and sit down," Patience said while looking at Sophia's bulging waistline.

"Let me go check on Richie," Sophia said as she walked out of the kitchen. She found Richie in the family room watching TV.

He beckoned her to sit beside him. "I have been waiting for you."

"I dashed to the kitchen to chat with Mum, though everyone thinks I am too heavy to stand on my feet."

"That's interesting. Did they say that?"

"Oh no, just my interpretation from the glances I received from the kitchen staff."

Richie smoothed a hand round Sophia's stomach. "Forgive them. They are eagerly waiting for the time they will include baby food on the house menu." Both broke into laughter.

"Did I ever mention to you how nice Mum is? Sophia chuckled. "I am still waiting to encounter the 'mother-in-law' that many people talk about."

They laughed again before Richie spoke. "I am not saying this because she is my mother, and a sweet mother she is to all of us, but many people find her caring and forgiving. Ask the workers …, ask Dad."

Sophia leaned over and kissed him. "I agree with you, up to now."

Richie encircled a hand around her waist. "I hope she is not competing with my love for you," he said as he leaned over and rested his head between her neck and shoulder.

"A mother's love is totally different, and better for daughters-in-laws," she said as she put a hand under his chin and lifted his head off her shoulder. "Listen, this will make you more envious. She is preparing my favourite dish, ugali. Do you want some tea, or we go out for a walk?"

Richie stood and offered her a hand. "Whichever you choose, I will follow."

She held onto his hand as he helped her to her feet. They left the house through the kitchen door. As soon as he noted the cool temperatures outside, Richie touched her bare arms. "I will bring you a sweater or a *kikoy*, to chase away the evening chilly wind."

As Sophia's pregnancy progressed, now at four months, Richie had become overly concerned regarding her wellbeing. He went out of his way, seeking to help her with daily activities that she could still perform without any discomfort. Always asking if he could help her while she took a bath, if she needed him to scrub her back, her feet or help her stand up from a chair.

On some days, before leaving for work in the morning, he reminded Theresa to check on Sophia, in case she needed help to get ready for her day.

When they went to Dr. Rajur for her prenatal visits, Richie asked more questions than Sophia did. Some questions she would have never thought of asking.

On some occasions, Sophia had to plead with Richie to stop studying books on pregnancy and parenthood. He read the books and wondered why she took the details he shared with her so lightly.

At one point, she almost convinced him when she said that women were born with some of the knowledge he struggled to understand from books. On further prodding, she explained that her mother, mother-in-law, and Justine her friend, provided answers to her questions on pregnancy and birth.

Sophia leaned against the wall of the house while she waited for Richie to return. Minutes later, he reappeared and wrapped a lime-green *kikoy* around her shoulders before he took one step back and slid his arms into his sweater.

Richie crooked an elbow and Sophia held on. "Thank you for the *kikoy,* though it will get me into a sweat. I'm already warm in my sleeveless dress."

"Just stay covered in case of a wandering mosquito or other evening insects. What did the doctor call them?" He asked as they turned right towards the orchard within the compound.

Sophia's thoughts drifted off. She asked herself how many women in the city or country had the leisure of taking an evening walk. Better still, within a well-fenced and guarded compound, with nothing to worry about except for a roving mosquito. Though, from popular stories, Nairobi was too cool for mosquitoes to thrive.

Sensing that Sophia was lost in thought, Richie squeezed her hand. "Want some fruit? I can stretch and pluck some, or even climb a tree, just for you."

He saw her face beam. Encouraged that he had her full attention, he said, "I booked a place in Naivasha for our getaway next week."

"I hope you have not paid," she said without turning to make eye contact.

Richie stopped and loosened her grip on his elbow. He took two steps ahead and stood in front of her. "Does that mean you would not like to take a break, go out of the city for some fresh air?"

She tilted her chin upwards and made eye contact. "What if I am not able to leave the office next week?"

"Thursday being a holiday, please take Wednesday and Friday off. We can come back on Sunday or Monday or stay longer if you want."

She walked on. "Let us go, we—"

Richie interrupted her with a cuddle and kissed her. "Thank you very much. I knew that, just like me, you would need a break away from the city."

She disentangled herself from his hold. "I wish you had waited for me to complete the sentence. What I meant is we continue walking, the reason that brought us outside. I doubt if going to Naivasha will be that easy." She held onto his hand. "Remember, it is only a few weeks ago since I stopped being unwell. I will need to ask the doctor and Mum first."

Richie stopped and kicked an apple on the ground, below an apple tree. He bent, picked it up and aimed it at birds on a nearby tree, scaring them into flight. He was thoughtful before he spoke in a lowered voice. "I called the doctor before confirming the booking. Dr. Rajur said so long as we do not race over potholes, or run down the rifts and valleys in Naivasha, it is perfectly okay."

As he uttered one word after another, Sophia resolved that she would not go on the Safari, though she would have appreciated a holiday before her pregnancy advanced further and limited her travels.

She turned to Richie. Her lips parted, but no words came out. She had wanted to ask why he contacted the doctor without asking her first. Why he did not give her a chance to contribute, even on a matter that directly concerned her.

Richie noticed the self-pity in her eyes and panicked. He juggled words in his mind on what to say to her. Before he could utter a word, she held and squeezed his hand tightly as her eyelids closed, like she was trying to shut out some pain. "You better have a convincing answer. I will tell Mum what you did without consulting me."

Richie crossed arms on his chest. "My mistake, I will call and cancel the booking," he said in a pleading voice as he let his hands drop to his side. "I really need a break from the city and supposed you would be happy to come with me."

She tightened her grip on his arm. For a moment, she felt sorry for uttering the words about reporting him to his mother, knowing that he did not take her words lightly. She had once heard Patience rebuke him when he went to the dining room, leaving her in the bedroom.

Sophia was quiet and thoughtful, considering what to say next. She was trying to get the right words, words which would rebuke and soothe him, all at once.

She reflected on how demanding his office work had been in the last two months, as he worked towards the launch of the new department by October. She felt pity on him, that on some days he worked a double shift, focusing on the new department, and fulfilling his tasks as a manager.

Sophia had once asked him to resign his managerial position to focus on the new department. To which he had explained that leaving his managerial position would leave him without a salary. The company directors had given only operating funds for the first six months, which meant he would work two jobs for one pay, until the new department started to generate income.

Sophia knew she needed to say something before the tears in her eyes poured out. Thoughts of him being without a salary had touched the core of her heart, reminding her how tough life had been for her before her employment as a PA. She had spent six months searching for a job in vain. "I will come with you. I hope a Safari to

Naivasha will be just that, one- or two-hours' drive from here."

"Please say nothing if tears drop out of my eyes. They are tears of joy." He said.

They were together on the topic of tears. Sophia felt her eyes turn moist. Her hope was that Richie would not look at her and notice her watery eyes.

They walked hand-in-hand without making eye contact.

As they approached the house from the left side, Richie squeezed Sophia's hand. When she paused and turned her eyes to him, he lifted his chin towards the main door to the house. "There comes Dad. Thanks for forgiving me. Mum would have mentioned the complaint to him, and I wouldn't know how to answer his questions."

Sophia squeezed his hand, assuring him that she would not report him. She decided she would apply for the two days' off from the office. But first, she needed to check her office diary and confirm with Michael that there were no urgent tasks that might hold her back.

She would also call doctor Rajur to confirm if it was safe for her to travel. On further thought, she decided there was no need to call the doctor since Richie had called. Instead, she would inform Patience of their intended travel. Sophia was certain that Patience would make it her homework to contact the doctor about her travel.

Satisfied with her plan, she asked, "Another round of walking, or do we leave the grounds for the dogs?"

"We will come back tomorrow." He supported the idea of going back to the house. He did not like it when the dogs jumped at Sophia and licked her hands. In the recent past, she had put her fear of dogs aside and would pet them without end. His concern was that after the dogs licked her hands, she might forget and touch her mouth or eyes.

He loved the three family guard dogs, but was afraid they might transfer germs to Sophia, "into her delicate body," as Dr. Rajur liked to say.

Chapter 14

Sophia was glad they took the advice from Patience to travel early Wednesday morning. There would be many cars on the road later in the day, with many people going upcountry for the long weekend.

They traveled in the family Volvo. A second car followed behind, a Range Rover driven by Nathan, one of the two security men who appeared whenever Richie or Michael traveled out of the country.

Sophia wondered how she would spend five days without a computer and her usual PA tasks. Other than clothes and other personal items, she had carried her cell phone and a book to read.

Richie too had left work behind, except for his phone, which she noted he had not looked at since they left the city.

As they branched off the main Nairobi-Nakuru highway onto a murram road, she wondered what type of hotel they were going to stay at, but she did not ask. Her guess was that since Patience allowed her to travel, it must have met her uncompromisingly high standards.

After about forty minutes of a slow drive, the scenery changed from short shrubs into a forested area. As the two cars came to a stop, two uniformed guards appeared and conversed with the drivers. After a safety inspection of the vehicles, the guards saluted as the gates opened, and the cars drove into the Sanctuary Country Club.

The cars parked in front of three houses in the shape of African round huts. Two of the houses were of comparable size and a third one much larger.

Richie helped Sophia out of the car and together with Nathan, they walked into the largest house. Two staff of the Country Club carried their bags inside.

Nathan and Richie conversed in low voices before Nathan left, closing the door behind him.

Richie followed Sophia who appeared to be inspecting the living room. On a bent knee, he extended his right hand to her. "May I have the pleasure of giving you a tour of this place?"

She smiled, revealing the dimples that had first attracted his attention to her while they were students at university.

He returned her smile. "There is a rumour that many presidents and other VIPs have spent their days and nights here."

She placed a hand on her chest. "Let's choose a country and pretend to be their leader, here on holiday."

"That will spoil our holiday. Those leaders never take a break, always worrying about policy, dissidents and angry publics," he said as they walked from the living room into a study area before entering the sleeping quarters. There were two bedrooms, a smaller one within the larger one.

A king-size poster bed took up about a quarter of the space in the larger bedroom. Four poles rising from the corners of the bed provided a beautiful canopy that supported the mosquito netting. The bed coverings, window curtains and other items in the room were all pleasantly coordinated into a beautiful cream and black ensemble.

Sophia could not recall ever seeing such beauty, even at furniture showrooms in the city. "I have no doubt about this being a holiday place for very, very important people - presidents." She smoothed her hand on the glass top of a coffee table at one end of the bedroom. "My only wish is they carried away all their paperwork, because we are not here for any policy formulation ventures." She stood on her toes and kissed Richie. "What are we doing here?" she asked while holding onto his waist.

"Because we are VVIPs, with important decisions to make, let's do this—"

Sophia looked at him, expectantly, waiting to gain sight of whatever he was referring to as this. He completed the sentence. "Extend our honeymoon here, this time with our baby."

Her dimples sank deeper. "I am still tongue-tied, that hidden in a forested area is such a splendid place. I am sure we will make it a pleasant and memorable stay," she said, snuggling into his chest, resting her head on his shoulder.

"After we have had a rest, I will take you to see the hundreds of rooms that make up this Club. On Friday, I will take you out to a golf tournament, a competition that draws enthusiasts from all over the country, and sometimes beyond," Richie said enthusiastically.

Sophia sat on one of the two chairs in the room. "That sounds like a nice joke, that there are even twenty, let alone hundreds of rooms in this Club, where?"

"Good, I'm happy that I have enough places to take you for your daily physical exercise."

~~~~~~

They returned to their house after having a buffet lunch, which had been set outside, under a large tent. Sophia lay down on the queen-size bed in the smaller bedroom since Richie insisted that she needed a siesta before her evening walk.

The next time she woke up, he was holding her hand, prodding her to get up and go for a walk while the sun was still up.

As they walked further away from their clubhouse, Sophia looked back, over her shoulder to register the location of their house. Nathan, walking a short distance behind them waved at her and she returned his greeting.

Richie squeezed her hand. "Nathan will be with us most of the time."

"Why?"
~~~~~~

He did not answer. Instead, he held her hand and they walked down a path, past houses of varied sizes, some single, others arranged in groups of threes and fives.

They came across a large set of houses where Richie stopped and pointed. "The layout of that village forms into a map of Africa when viewed from above." They marveled at the arrangement before walking on.

As they started to descend a concrete stairway, Sophia paused in her step. "I don't think we should go farther. Did I not hear you mention wild animals?"

"By now we would have seen warning signs all over the walkway," he tried to reassure her.

She pulled her hand free from his. "Not today," as she turned to face the direction from which they had come.

Richie looked down the slope. "You are right, we can come back another day, maybe when there will be group guided tours."

She did not reveal that she was more concerned about missing a step and falling down the steep valley, than an encounter with wild animals. She had read in one of her prenatal books that simple falls were a major cause of miscarriages, especially in the first and second trimesters.

They walked back, past their house and stopped at a swimming pool. There were close to fifty people, including children, at the pool.

"Hi Richie," a man called out. Sophia turned her head to follow the voice and saw Richie shake hands with a man they had once met at a club in the city.

Sophia extended her hand to the woman next to the man, "Sophia, Richie's wife."

"Josephine, Patrick's wife," she responded before focusing her attention to the swimming pool. "My three-year-old insisted on entering the pool. I must not turn my eyes from her for long."

The four sat on poolside chairs and chatted enthusiastically, from their decisions to leave the city over the long weekend to the forthcoming golf tournament.

As time passed, more people joined in the free-flowing conversation, many of whom Richie appeared to be familiar with. Later, the group walked into a large rotunda where they ate dinner.

At around 9:00pm, Richie excused himself from the group and walked away with Sophia and Nathan.

Richie was hopeful, having seen Sophia happy and chatty most of the evening. He looked forward to a positive conversation with her that night about her employment.

After a bath, Sophia hugged Richie. "My day has been good. I will retire for the night if you promise to hold me tight."

Could Richie object to the invitation, though it conflicted with his plan to talk with Sophia about her job?

Chapter 15

"Today, not even food will get me out of this bed." Sophia proclaimed as she peeped from under the Egyptian cotton bed sheet covering her head.

She slowly uncovered her head and looked at Richie as he entered the bedroom, a white towel hanging from one shoulder. He had just returned from a morning exercise in the gym in their clubhouse.

He wiped sweat from his forehead with the towel. "Did I hear you mention food? I am with you on that."

"I said I feel tired. I just want to stay in bed."

He took long strides to reach the bed, bent, and held her hand. "Is everything okay? Did we make you too tired from watching the golf tournament yesterday?"

"Whatever. The only thing I know is that I will not leave this room today."

He threw the towel on the floor and drew the mosquito net to one side of the bed, then placed the back of his hand on Sophia's cheek, then her forehead. "You have no temperature. Please sit upright."

She pulled the bed sheet up to her neck while explaining to Richie that she was fine, not sick, only tired.

He pulled the duvet over her shoulders before stretching to reach his phone on the bedside table. "I will call the resident doctor and ask if we need to go to hospital."

She pushed away the bed coverings, pulled herself into a sitting position and held his hand. "Please. Let's discuss this first. I feel helpless whenever you make decisions for me." She threw both hands into the air. "I only voiced my wish to stay in bed. Did that sound like I am unwell?"

"You never know," he said as he replaced his phone on the table. "Let's go for our morning bath, after which we can call the doctor, or Mum, whichever you choose."

Sophia was annoyed that Richie had reached a conclusion that she was unwell and decided on whom they needed to consult for guidance.

She recollected well, that earlier on, even before the vomiting which landed her at the doctor's clinic started, she had been feeling tired, especially in the early morning. She recalled how the tiredness had transformed her from an early morning person, into one who needed multiple nudging of the alarm clock to get out of bed.

It then dawned on her that Richie was not aware of her morning struggles. On weekdays, he left the bedroom before her first wake-up call. On weekends, they were never in a hurry to wake up, which meant her wanting to sleep more was new to him.

The realization evoked anger in her. Richie's absence on her weekday mornings meant he had missed seeing her new reality, which he now construed as illness.

She stepped out of bed and walked away into the bathroom.

He followed her as she spoke. "I will still stay in the room because I feel tired, but I am not sick."

"What about our baby?"

She paused and looked at him over her shoulder. "That is a part of me, I guess. When I say I, I'm referring to the whole of me," she waved a hand from her face downwards. "With the baby, I would for sure tell the difference between being unwell and tired."

"I will take your word." Richie entered the bathroom, picked her toothbrush from the holder, added toothpaste and handed the brush to her.

She accepted the brush. "Thank you," one side of her mouth twisted upwards into a forced smile.

He pulled a bathroom stool closer to her. She looked at it before pushing it away with her leg. "Thank you," and started to brush her teeth besides one of the three sinks in the bathroom.

Richie took a shower while Sophia relaxed in the adjacent Jacuzzi.

He was thoughtful, and finally decided he would call for room service to save her the bother of walking to the dining room.

Richie dressed in grey sports trousers and a white t-shirt that clung, revealing his muscular chest and arms. He walked into the study room, pressed a button on the room phone and talked with Nathan.

When Sophia was ready, she picked a scarf and covered her shoulders. "You must be starving after your early morning exercise. Let's go eat."

"I decided to save you energy. I called for—"

The doorbell rang before he could complete the sentence. He held her hand before he let it go as his phone buzzed. He answered the phone by saying one word, "Okay."

The main door opened.

Sophia, who had walked into the study area, stared at Richie.

He read the panicky expression on her face and explained, "They have brought us breakfast," as he extended his left hand to her.

They walked into the sitting room as two hotel staff walked out of the house. Nathan stayed back. After a brief chat with Richie, Nathan flipped a key card on the sensor of their door then walked out and closed the door behind him.

Richie followed Sophia into the dining room while in a monologue. "We can now take our time to eat and stay indoors."

He saw the expression on her face, one cheek pushed upwards in a questioning manner. He leaned his head closer to her ear and whispered, "Rules to follow whenever we are far away from home."

He sat on the chair next to Sophia and held her hand while he kissed her on the cheek. "Nothing much to worry about except being away from home, or rather, being

Mwasimba family." He forced a cough. "A businessman, a successful one by some people's standards, means some things are done differently."

Sophia placed two cups on the table and served tea. "You are confusing me even more."

Richie picked a teaspoon. "This house is mostly used by dignitaries, so the lock is in such a way that our person, Nathan, has access. That's the reason he phoned me before he opened the door."

Sophia paused from serving tea. She put the kettle on the table and looked at Richie.

He sensed that she needed to hear more. "He will never just walk in unless I allow him to, as I did after he alerted me before opening the door. Okay?"

She picked the tea kettle and placed it on her opposite end of the table. She was reflective. She wanted to ask Richie why the Mwasimba family allowed themselves to live in fear. She wanted to tell him that a holiday was more enjoyable without Nathan or the driver following them everywhere.

On further thought, she decided that could be how the rich lived - in fear - hence the security people following them everywhere. Pressing Richie for more information could reveal how little she knew about the lives of rich people. "Thank goodness," she said as she placed a plate of fried eggs in front of Richie.

She picked up a croissant for herself. "I am still in wonder, how they decided that we needed breakfast in the room."

"I called for it as you were getting dressed. I assumed you heard me."

Sophia's hand remained holding a cup of tea halfway to her mouth. "I need to jog my mind. I do not remember you asking me what I would have liked for breakfast." She sipped tea and replaced the cup on the table. "And, you must have mentioned all these items very fast." She waved her hands over the food items on the table.

Richie took a sip of his tea before he slowly cut a piece of the fried egg. He was in deep thought, juggling words in his mind, what else to tell Sophia.

He considered whether it was the right time and place to explain to Sophia the reason they were on holiday with Nathan, a trained bodyguard. And a driver who could respond equally well in case of an external threat.

After a short while, he decided he would explain that to her later, when they were back in the city. He had a different goal to achieve for the day, no need to add stories of potential and imagined security issues.

Richie's plan for the day was to make Sophia comfortable and happy to the extent that he would easily talk her into agreeing to resign from her job.

After one hour of eating while chatting, Sophia walked towards a bedroom next to the gym. "I like the way this house is designed, appears small from the outside, yet it is a complete house with all amenities."

"What our sister Joy would call a superior design of houses." Richie placed his hand on Sophia's shoulder.

"How is Joy fairing on with her job at the construction company?"

"As happy as ever, does she ever have reasons not to be happy?"

"Mama raised you guys well, always happy and grateful. I need to learn from you." He encircled his hand around her waist and guided her towards the gym. "This is where I left my energy in the morning. It means I will stay indoors with you today. Come, we'll watch TV." They went to the living room.

"Please, do not stay because of me. You are free to join one of the group Safaris for a tour of the game park. I will be okay by myself, watch TV and catch up on sleep." She explained.

He picked the remote and flipped through the television channels, though he was not keen on any of the programs. He was engrossed in thought, juggling words in his mind, trying to find the best way to tell Sophia there was no way he would leave her alone in the room and venture out into the game park, however much he would have wanted to go. "It's good you asked that we stay indoors." He cuddled and kissed her. "A reminder that I need a good rest, before we travel back to the city, rejuvenated." He was glad when he saw her smiley face.

He handed the TV remote to her. "It is your turn to select a channel for us to watch."

She held the remote, glad that he had given her a rare chance to decide on what they would watch together. She flipped through channels, stopping to read previews before moving to the next one.

Richie took advantage of her concentration on the TV channels to formulate a strategy. He needed to generate a strategy on the best way to introduce the topic of her resignation, without upsetting her.

Aware that Sophia was very qualified and wanted to further her career at work, he had to be careful with his choice of words. Having been classmates at the national university, he was aware she wanted to continue working, even with a baby on the way. It was going to be a huge challenge for him to convince her to resign from her job.

"Did you fall asleep on the sofa?" Sophia asked as she softly elbowed Richie's arm.

"Looks like I will be the first one back in bed, ahead of you," he said, forcing a smile.

By midday they had watched two movies, a family comedy, and a Christian musical, and golf. All were Sophia's choice.

Chapter 16

After lunch Sophia and Richie took a leisurely walk to the well-tended fruit orchard within the expansive grounds of the Country Club.

A woman in a khaki uniform dress welcomed them. "My name is Grace." She touched the name tag on her chest. "Welcome to our earthly garden of Eden. You may pick fruits of your choice to eat." She handed over small reed baskets, one to Richie, Sophia, and Nathan.

"Are they sprayed with any chemicals?" Sophia asked as she reached a short hedge of strawberries.

"We pride ourselves on having a natural environment, more so since we are located within a national park. Everything we do aims to protect our visitors and the environment for the wildlife." She harvested two strawberries and stuffed them into her mouth.

Each filled their baskets and left for their house. On arrival, Sophia excused herself and went to lie down on the bed while Richie and Nathan played a board game.

After two hours, Nathan left as Richie went to wake Sophia up. "I doubt you have any sleep left for the night, though that will be good for me."

"I have a ton of sleep. I could sleep for twenty hours," she sat upright on the bed as her feet touched the carpeted floor. "Were it not for my husband who gets panicky." She stood, stretched with an audible yawn before walking off to the bathroom.

Richie watched her walk away. He liked how elegant she looked wearing one of the night dresses he had bought for her most recently. He had made it a habit of buying her sleeping attire every fourth night. He planned to continue unless she chose to top him.

He was happy with what she had said about being very tired and ready to sleep for more hours. Her words gave him the impetus he needed to continue the conversation they had started after breakfast, regarding her constant need for a rest. His hope was to use this to convince her to stay home and sleep as much as she needed.

"Are you ready to get back to bed?" He asked as she emerged from the bathroom.

"Is that a challenge? You know I will win. Sleep now, and still sleep at night."

Richie smiled, it was now or never, the moment he had been waiting for had presented itself. All he needed was to say what had been bothering him for months now.

He encircled both hands around her waist and held her in front of him, her back to his chest. Supporting her like a child learning to take their first steps, he guided her to a nearby two-seater sofa, both sat down. "The only knowledge I have about pregnancy is from you. It must be a tiring stage of life with beautiful results, of course."

Sophia leaned sideways, rested her head on his shoulder. "Pregnancy is something you would never understand and so you should stop panicking about, especially when I say I want to stay in bed forever."

Richie nuzzled her closer to his chest. "I cannot pretend to understand it the way you do, but I fully appreciate what you said." He kissed her. "Please consider resigning from work, that way you will have enough time to rest. We will manage financially, I promise. I have the funds we need."

Sophia struggled out of his hold. "I cannot imagine a life without my job."

"Even for the sake of your health?" he asked.

She shook her head.

He embraced her back to his chest. "I'm not saying you are unwell. If you stay home, you will be able to wake up only when you want to, and sleep whenever you feel like." He stroked her hair to her face and backwards. "And you could go with Mum to the mall for your daily walks, or wherever you like, to do shopping."

"I have seen women work to the last day of their pregnancy. There is no reason for me to stop working," she retorted.

There was silence in the room. Richie was busy stringing ideas together on what to say next without getting her more agitated.

Sophia was reflective. She thought of her mother and the many women in the village who worked the cultivated fields while pregnant. The next day, there would be news that so and so delivered a healthy baby in the night.

She thought of how she had seen her mother get back to cooking for the family, cleaning the house, and bathing her younger children hardly a week after she delivered Babu, her last-born brother.

Sophia thought of how comfortable her life was, and how she had no reason to stop going to work. She had access to a driver whenever she needed to go somewhere, so waking up and being chauffeured to and from the office was not strenuous. Stress would be riding in a matatu to and from the office, though most of the women in the city still did that while pregnant.

Richie smoothed Sophia's stomach. He was thoughtful, wondering how to share with her the turmoil in his mind.

He would have liked to tell her that his mother got satisfaction from staying home to raise her five sons while his father toiled away every day, building the family business. The result was a happy father, a happy mother, and happy children. He wanted the same lifestyle for her, and for their children.

He frantically sought words to tell her that he wanted to be the financial provider for his family. She would stay home and take care of their children and him, whenever he arrived home tired, or needed comforting. He yearned for her to know that the tasks he had seen his mother perform as a stay-at-home mother were quite enough for any one person. It was going to be a burden for Sophia to work as a PA while managing their family. In addition, he could afford to support his family financially, without having her in employment.

He wondered how to explain to Sophia that his mother staying home was one of the most significant contributions to the success of his father at work, and of the children at school... and the effective management of the workers within the family home – including drivers and the security personnel.

Richie knew of many children from rich families who had gone astray in life, partly because of having parents who were too busy at work, never at home to provide the companionship and guidance needed by growing children. He so much wanted Sophia to understand the same - that if she stayed home, he would have little to worry about her or the family's wellbeing. Consequently, he would focus all his energy on the very demanding business responsibilities.

Sophia stood up and walked away. Richie followed her into the sitting room. She sat and picked the TV remote as he sat next to her and asked. "Want to talk? I really want to hear you say that you will resign and take a deserved rest while we wait for our baby."

"I am not unwell and hence I have no need to stay at home," she said while moving away from him.

"You are not sick, but you need a different pace, with more rest, and more sleep, as you indicated this morning and after lunch."

Richie was irritated that in the morning Sophia did not want to get out of bed because she was tired. After lunch, she slept for two hours. Now, she was refusing the very logical and reasonable offer to stay home and get enough rest.

His fingers involuntarily drummed the armrest of the sofa. He worried and fretted about what people would think of him, of his father and the company, if Sophia went to an official meeting and dozed off after lunch.

Richie involuntarily folded a fist and hit the armrest. He only realized what he had done when Sophia switched off the TV and turned his direction.

He leaned forward, rested his forehead on his left hand. "Sorry. I got scared when I imagined you dozing off at an official meeting, and people start to wonder if you were forced to go to work." He stood and went to the kitchen and returned with two bottles of water. He handed one to her and placed the second one on the coffee table before walking to the bathroom next to the gym.

Sophia went to the kitchen where she washed fruits from one of the two baskets and placed them on a kitchen towel before arranging them on a plate. She balanced the plate on one hand and went back to the sitting room.

She picked two strawberries and held them in her hand, without putting them in the mouth. She reflected on what Richie said, worried if she would one day fall asleep at work. She smiled, remembering what she had read in one of her books on prenatal care. One way to avoid exhaustion was to eat little amounts of food at short intervals. Eating one large meal strained the digestive system, the reason many expectant women needed to rest or even sleep after eating.

Richie returned and sat next to her. She noticed that he had washed his face. She held his hand in hers. "I am sorry," She kissed him. "But I will go on working. I will stop if I feel overwhelmed by sleep."

"What if you consider resigning before that happens, before getting overwhelmed?"

"That will not happen. Right now, my body knows we are on holiday, the reason it wants to sleep all the time. I will be okay when back to the normal work routine."

Richie picked an apple and bit into it. He was thoughtful. He almost broke into a smile, figuring that from what he had noticed since their arrival in Naivasha, Sophia would need to sleep even more once they were back in the city. She would soon voluntarily resign from her job.

He spoke without looking at her. "Please, I hope you know that you can give a short notice to leave work, whenever the need arises." He cuddled her. "And I will come drive you home."

She laughed aloud. "I had no idea someone could leave work so unceremoniously. I will give proper notice if I need to stop working."

"To tell you the truth, you have worked with the company long enough, in terms of years, and you have given your best. You do not need to labour more." He supported her head and levelled their foreheads. "The Mwasimba Company has a reputation and prides itself on the welfare of its employees." He freed her head.

He nibbled on the apple before he spoke again. "My good guess is that Chairman would be happy with a one-minute notice to resign. He would be devastated to hear that an employee collapsed at work because they were afraid to give a short notice, so as to go for a deserved rest."

"Okay," Sophia said.

Richie became more attentive, waiting to hear if the okay meant that she would resign from work. He listened as she spoke. "I will take leave if I feel overwhelmed. I am not resigning from my PA position, unless the company does not allow women to work then go on maternity leave."

Richie stood up abruptly and took a glance at his Rolex. He extended a hand to her. "Let us go for a walk, it will do both of us a lot of good."

They exited the house and met with Nathan outside. The trio strolled casually towards a forested area near the main entrance to the club. They returned an hour later, everyone in a happy mood as they went to the dining room for dinner.

When Richie and Sophia retired back into their house, Sophia held onto his hand. "Is it okay if we travel back tomorrow? I guess you have had the rest and rejuvenation you needed away from the city."

Richie exhaled, audibly. "I was waiting to hear more pleasant words, like you will go to the office on Monday to hand in your letter of resignation."

"I am not resigning. I want to work for my money."

He held her tenderly by the shoulder. "The Amex card I gave you is for your use, for all your money needs. Let me know if you prefer cash." He massaged her shoulders while he asked, "What time do you prefer we leave tomorrow, though we can stay here longer?"

Sophia's shoulders relaxed from the impromptu massage she was getting. "Eleven o'clock should be an appropriate time to travel."

"Good," he said as he fetched his cell phone from his trouser pocket. He pressed one button on the phone and replaced it into the pocket. A few minutes later Nathan opened the front door to their house.

Sophia walked away, leaving the two men in conversation. She went and took a shower instead of her usual bath. She was in the bedroom reading a book when Richie entered and closed the door behind him.

While showering, Richie was reflective of what he had achieved during their days away from the city. Not much. Next, he wished that Sophia would doze off on her first day back to work, and then be compelled to voluntarily resign.

By the time he walked into the bedroom, he had decided he would talk with Michael, hint to him that Sophia would resign any time soon. The thought brought comfort to his heart. He was glad she had asked that they return to the city the next day.

He looked forward to Monday. He pictured himself arriving home after work to some good news that Sophia was too tired to get out of bed, or that she had dozed off while at work and had given a short notice to vacate her PA post.

After the soothing thought, Richie went to bed for the night, happy. He hugged his wife as he dozed off. He was at peace.

Chapter 17

It was mid-September, and Sophia was still working as a PA to Michael. She had vehemently turned down a less demanding job within the company.

To her surprise, she noted that she was becoming more energetic as her pregnancy progressed. On some days, she got out of bed in the morning before Richie left for work.

Richie interpreted her renewed energy differently. Sophia was over-pushing herself for him to see that she no longer needed to stop going to work.

One week before Richie was to travel to three African countries, he brought up the topic of Sophia's resignation again.

"Please apply for leave during the time I will be away."

"I am fine enough to go to work. I need to save all my leave days, then use them to extend the period of my maternity leave."

Richie was running out of ideas on how to convince Sophia to resign from her PA post. He decided to consult other people for fresher ideas.

One day, he went for lunch with Patty to Truphena Towers, another landmark building in the city owned by the Mwasimba Group of Companies. While there, he asked if she could talk with Sophia, convince her to resign.

By the end of their two-hour lunch, Richie had shared some of the steps he had taken and not succeeded.

Patty confessed that she could not think of any other approach, nor would she talk with Sophia on her resignation. Patty explained that though her friendship with Sophia went way back, the situation would be awkward because Richie was her cousin, while Sophia was her good friend, and now her sister-in-law.

After lunch, Richie picked some documents on the new department and left the office for the day. He arrived home before 3:00pm, changed into gym clothes and exercised in the home gym for one hour.

He overstayed in the shower, doing nothing other than letting water flow over his body. Thereafter, he went to the home library to prepare for his travel in three days' time.

Richie did not achieve much while in the library, spending time juggling ideas in his mind. At one point he thought of asking Sophia to take leave and travel with him for the ten days he would be away.

He shelved the idea, realizing she would not agree. She had talked of reserving her leave days for later. Further, he also didn't know what he would do if she became ill while on travel. That would force him to shorten his trip and return home. He also worried over what might happen if a doctor advised against travel back home until after the baby was born.

Not wanting to entertain the disturbing thought of Sophia becoming sick while away in a foreign country, he heard words escape from his mouth. "Better if she is home. Mum will handle any emergency." Concerned that someone might have heard his words, he surveyed the library to be sure there was no one around.

He ambled from one bookshelf to the next, not searching for any specific book until the sound of the library door opening startled him, alerting him of the presence of his mother as she asked. "Are you not taking Sophia for a walk today? I see she is waiting by the family room."

"I am not feeling well. We can do that tomorrow morning," he said without turning in her direction.

"Are both of you not going to work tomorrow?"

"I will work from home. I am not sure if Sophia will agree to stay."

Patience must have sensed that Richie was not ready to engage in further conversation. She walked away, paused at the door, and asked if he would join them for tea.

"Not soon. I need to find what I am looking for," he said as he touched books on the shelf and pulled out a magazine on landscaping.

He was relieved when he heard the door close, a sign that his mother had left the library. Noting the topic of the magazine, he returned it and went to the shelf with books and journals on finance and money markets where he pulled out a journal without checking the title or date of publication.

Richie mulled over whether to join Patience and Sophia for tea. While there he could voice his concerns about Sophia. He abandoned the idea, reminding himself that Sophia would not take kindly to being discussed in the presence of his mother.

Better to send a message to Sophia, letting her know he would skip the tea. He saw that he had two missed calls from her, one at four o'clock and the second one an hour later. He typed a response. "Hi Sunshine, sorry I missed your calls, I was in the gym, then the library. I will come over for dinner."

A minute later, he read her response. "Okay."

He read the message three times, stood up and paced the library floor, pondering what she meant by the one word, okay. He had hoped she would join him in the library, a chance for him to tell her how bothered he was that she would be going to work while he was out of the country.

At 7:30pm, Richie put back all the books he had pulled from the bookshelves and walked out of the library. He decided it was better to appear at the dinner table before Sophia or his mother came to call him.

If his mother came to the library, he would be forced to explain whatever was troubling him. He was not so sure if he wanted to share his concerns with her, knowing that she would consult Sophia on the issue. He did not want that to happen, as Sophia might renew her earlier call for them to move to their own house.

Richie forced a smile as he approached the dining table. He was both concerned and happy to see his father. He worried that everyone had been waiting for him, but glad that he had left the library of his own will, and hence, he had no reason to give an excuse for his late arrival.

During dinner, he had a brief discussion with his father about the new department.

"You must be looking forward to your travels to establish what others are doing and identify gaps we could fill or take advantage of," Mwasimba stated while looking at Richie.

" Sometimes, I am happy, then apprehensive the rest of the time."

"Why is that?" Patience asked.

"It has to do with new things, new situations." He waved his hand in defeat. "I will overcome all, soon." The family ate almost in silence, except for brief chats on the food, the weather and anecdotal effects of the recent political elections on their business.

After dinner Richie excused himself, explaining that preparing for the travel had sapped all his energy. He needed to sleep if he was to work effectively the next day. He wished his parents a goodnight, kissed Sophia on the cheek and walked away.

~ ~ ~ ~ ~

Sophia was astonished by Richie's uncharacteristic behaviour. She could not remember another time when he had kissed her good night at the dining table, or anywhere else since their marriage. He always wished everyone else a goodnight, but not her. They would always meet in the bedroom for a heart-to-heart talk and a prayer before they retired for the night.

On realizing that Patience was looking at her, Sophia stood and wished her in-laws a good night and followed Richie.

She was surprised to find that within the few minutes she had stayed back at the table, Richie had brushed his teeth and was in bed. "Already in bed, how was your shower?"

"I had my shower when I arrived home, long before bells rang for the end of the school day."

"Interesting, that means I have a long way to catch up with you." Sophia said as she went and selected a nightie.

Richie pulled a sheet over his head. "Wake me up in case I drift off to sleep, or we can talk tomorrow. I will be home."

"Oh! Are you unwell?" She walked closer to the bed.

"Not really, only tired from over-thinking about my travel. I will miss you. I will be out of the country while you will be at work, and that bothers me, scares me."

"No need to worry about me. I will be here with Mum, Dad, Michael, and the rest of the family. I am the one who will worry while you are away, alone." She kissed him on the forehead and walked off to the bathroom.

He was fast asleep when she returned. She pulled a bed sheet over her head while reflecting on what could be troubling Richie about travel, especially for a project he was most excited about. She could not recall ever seeing him this disturbed before.

Sophia awoke to her morning alarm and was surprised to see Richie fast asleep. Not wanting to wake him up, she tiptoed out of the room to the bathroom.

He was still asleep as she dressed and left for breakfast. When she re-entered the bedroom, Richie was out of bed, and she could tell from the sound of a waterfall and a song, that he was enjoying his morning shower.

She pulled a Post-It pad and jotted. "Good morning. How was your night? See you later my love." She pasted the paper on the dresser mirror and left for the car waiting for her on the driveway.

Chapter 18

Richie made himself comfortable on his window seat and watched cartoons until he heard the announcement to get ready for landing at Oliver Tambo International Airport, Johannesburg, South Africa.

As he walked out of the plane, he thought of how peculiar his days away from home were going to be. Yet he needed to focus on his scheduled meetings, gather information he so much needed to make the new department a worthy addition. The success of the department would mean his promotion into the position of director, following which he would earn more money to support his growing family.

He stepped out of the plane, stood beside the entrance, and watched fellow passengers stream out until Nathan arrived. They walked together through customs, collected their checked luggage, and traveled to the hotel.

Richie felt more relaxed as he chatted with Nathan. There and then, he decided Nathan would be by his side throughout his visit. "Hey man," Richie called as he patted Nathan on the shoulder. "If you get bored, you may come sit in at my meetings."

"You want me to change my profession? I will think about your invitation."

Richie had a tight program with back-to-back meetings - with individuals, as well as with various groups. On most days, his schedule was filled up, from eight in the morning to seven or eight in the night.

He religiously made time to call Sophia every morning, lunchtime and at night. Whenever he had extra time in between, he called his mother and enquired about the rest of the family.

His last stop was in Kampala, Uganda, and it was a breeze. On the flight from Entebbe International Airport to Nairobi, Richie thought of the profitable business he had given to his cell phone service provider. He had maxed out the one-thousand-dollar monthly credit for his international calls. Something he had never done before. However, he felt okay with the expenditure. The calls to Sophia and to his mother provided the reassurances he needed while he focused on the assignment that took him to South Africa, Zambia, and Uganda.

He was happy with the achievements and findings from the meetings, and looked forward to the launch of the department, which was just three weeks away.

On the drive from the airport, he asked the driver to take him to the office first before home. His plan was to surprise Sophia.

When the elevator chimed 52nd floor of Akoth Towers, Richie was glad that Liz was not at the reception desk. He did not want anyone to delay his stride to Sophia's office.

He paused at Sophia's door and pressed the handle down. The door did not open. He hurried along the corridor and stopped at the next door emblazoned in gold: *Michael Mwasimba, Director, Marketing*. He knocked, opened the door, and walked inside.

"Welcome back. How was your multi-country trip?" Michael called out as he swiveled his chair away from his mahogany desk.

"The work side of my travel was good. I missed you guys," Richie said as he extended a hand to meet that of Michael.

"Understandable, considering you left your other half behind," Michael said as he sat down.

Richie made himself comfortable on one of the two visitors' chairs. "Good trip. I met with fantastic businesspeople. There are gaps for us to fill, and fabulous opportunities to take advantage of."

Michael rolled his chair farther back. "What I am hearing is that you are extremely enthusiastic. No time to take an after-travel rest?"

"I will write a detailed report soon, but first I need to find Sophia." He stood up and made eye contact with Michael.

"She was here in the morning but left after lunch. She mentioned something she needed to go do."

Richie pulled his phone from the breast pocket of his Zegna jacket, flipped through like he was looking for messages. He put the phone back into the pocket. "I see no missed calls. I will go find her."

He turned to leave as Michael spoke. "She could be home waiting for you." He chuckled and winked at Richie. "And here you are, talking about meetings and financial markets."

Richie grinned, bid Michael goodbye, and left. He arrived home just before 4:00 p.m. and hurried inside, only pausing to return a greeting from Theresa who had come to take his luggage inside.

Worry crept in as Richie took quick strides to the silent and still north wing. Sophia was not nearby. He paused at the bedroom door, took a deep breath before he pressed the handle and entered.

There she was ... fast asleep.

~~~~~~

As Richie stepped out of the shower, he was pleased that Sophia had been asleep when he arrived. The almost cold shower he preferred brought clarity to his mind as he pondered what could have made her leave the office before the end of the workday.

He ruled out illness. She would have called Patience and proceeded to the doctor's clinic. He tried to recall if he had caught any hidden message as Michael informed him that she had been at work in the morning. A smile appeared on his face, coincident with the thought that perhaps she could be very tired, and would thus write her letter of resignation when she woke up?
~~~~~~

While in the bedroom, he tiptoed, afraid that plodding his full one hundred and twenty kilograms on the floor could disrupt her sleep. He sneaked out of the bedroom, pulling the door behind him until it met the jamb without making a sound.

He went to the kitchen and greeted the house chef before he walked to the dining table and served tea.

After about thirty minutes of reflecting on his travel and what it meant for his future in terms of career and money, he saw Sophia at the family room, walking towards the dining room while rubbing her eyes, like she was struggling to have a better view of Richie.

He cleared her doubts when he took long strides and reached her, cuddled while he kissed her on the mouth and all over her face. "I now believe I am home after all those long days and nights without you," he said while cuddling her more.

"I missed you all the time." Sophia chocked on her words still rubbing her eyes.

Richie kissed her again before releasing her, "I missed you every minute I was away. I missed you more when I saw you sleeping peacefully."

"I wish you had woken me up," a teary Sophia said as she leaned on his shoulder.

She really had missed Richie in the ten days he had been away. Each night, before retiring to bed, she had spent time looking at their wedding photos.

She had also reflected on the time when Richie spent two days working from home, yet all she had done was wake up and leave for the office. She had admonished herself for not staying home so that they could spend more time together.

As the days of separation passed and Sophia's phone kept ringing with Richie's photo on her screen, she had comforted herself that he was indeed not upset with her. The reason she took the Thursday afternoon off was to welcome him back home.

Richie held her shoulders at arms' length and inspected her from head to toe. "I should not travel again. I see I missed to witness as our baby grew by more inches." He held her hand and they walked to the dining table, "Some tea for you? But if you are not very hungry, I prefer you prepare we go for a walk, or for an evening out."

Sophia tilted her head upwards. She inhaled a long puff of air, exhaled and said, "No nice aroma from the kitchen, it means Mum is not home yet. I will go for a change of clothes." She encircled her arms around Richie's neck, kissed him and walked away.

Richie fought a temptation to follow her. He decided it was better not to. His plan was to take her to the club, show their friends and other patrons how proud of her he was, as a soon to be father.

He called his mother and exchanged pleasantries, called his father, and briefed him on what he had determined from his fact-finding mission. He sent an SMS to Nick before he called Bill. As they got into an enchanted conversation, Sophia walked into the room dressed in a Stella McCartney dress and leather fur-lined Gucci loafers.

Richie walked towards her and snaked his hand on her back as he concluded the phone call with Bill, "Hey, bro. My best friend has just walked in, and she is gorgeous. Talk to you later." He ended the call and embraced Sophia.

They stepped outside. Sophia stood near the kitchen door while Richie walked to the garage and drove back in the Maserati, he had added to his fleet two months back. He held the passenger door for her before he got back in the driver's seat.

He sat quietly until she questioned. "Are we waiting for someone else?"

He placed a hand on her knee. "The evening is all yours. I am waiting for instructions on where you want to go drink tea and eat supper."

Sophia was thoughtful. She held her left pointer finger to one side of her mouth. "I would have liked to go to my favourite café in town, but I doubt we'll arrive on time, with all that traffic at this time of day. We could go to the restaurant at our local mall, but I guess everyone will be there, drinking tea as they wait for the evening traffic to clear."

Richie did not interrupt her. He sat massaging her knee and waited as she voiced the thoughts in her head.

She made eye contact. "Because of the traffic, we have nowhere but your famous destination, the nearby Karen club. We may go now," she said with a chuckle.

He winked at her before starting the car engine. He had wanted to embrace her and let her know that her choice of their destination would have been his choice as well. But he decided otherwise, he would keep his thoughts to himself. That way, she would be happy that going to the club was fully her choice.

~~~~~~

Sophia was surprised that there were many people at the club on a Thursday. She asked for tea-masala and a chocolate cake.

Richie made a coughing sound, to hold back the words he almost blurted out. He had wanted to ask her about sugar in the cake.

"What is so funny, that I have asked for cake?"

He had a mischievous smile, which faded as two ladies walked towards their table. The taller of the two held out open arms to Sophia. "Welcome back, glad you are finally back here, we did not scare you away with our happy song the last time you were here, did we?"

Sophia stood up to receive the embrace. She was taken aback when the lady paused her step, stood still with her arms and mouth wide open.

Sophia was confused by the reaction. She glanced at Richie.

All she saw was his happy face. She turned back to the lady and saw that she was inspecting Sophia's mid-body.

The lady made eye contact. "I do not want to go into history books as the girl who made you faint while
~~~~~~

carrying a Mwasimba baby. The club...," she waved her hand in the air. "All clubs will lock me out, as a danger to unborn babies." She embraced Sophia in a loose hug, like she was afraid of hurting her stomach.

Sophia broke into laughter then stopped abruptly. She disentangled from the embrace and extended her right hand to the second lady, who returned the greeting. "My name is Christine. Nice to see you again, Sophia. Had no idea I have not seen you for that long." She pointed to Sophia's stomach before she pulled up a nearby chair and sat.

Richie lifted his chin from one lady to the other. "Monnie, Chris, I am sad that there is no greeting for me."

Monica sighed. "If I faint, you will be the one to blame. I am still tongue-tied at how active you guys have been in bed."

Sophia's eyes opened wide until there was no more skin for them to bulge out. She looked at Christine, instead of Monica who had voiced a statement she found displeasing. She turned Richie's direction when she heard him speak. "Monnie, I encourage you to get serious with that boyfriend of yours. Nothing can compare to the happiness hidden in marriage."

He winked at Sophia and lifted her hand to his mouth before he turned to Monica. "As you have seen, Sophia and I are pregnant, fully into it and enjoying it."

Christine's lips parted, like she wanted to say something but stopped when Richie held a hand in front of her.

"Hope you have no more to add. We are expecting our first of many babies, and we are filled with joy."

The muscles on Sophia's face loosened into a smile.

Richie added, "What if you join in the celebration?" He beckoned a waiter to their table.

Monica and Christine turned and locked eyes, but none uttered a word.

Having grown up with Monica and Christine, often bumping into one another at school, and later at the various clubs and hallways of high-end shopping malls, Richie knew it was his responsibility to stop them from making jokes about Sophia's pregnancy. Since Sophia was not familiar with them and their funny side, she might not take it kindly.

Monica scrutinized Sophia. "We were headed to the bar, but we can start with tea if our brother here insists."

Sophia returned the gaze. "We are happy to have you here for tea. As my dear husband just said, we are celebrating very many blessings. You are welcome to join us."

The four got busy chatting on many general topics, from improvements made to two other clubs, to being out at that early hour of the evening. Later, two men joined them - dates for Monica and Christine.

By the time Sophia and Richie walked off into the dining section of the club, Sophia was happy that Monica and Christine had joined them for tea. She now had enough details on them. They were great friends, could qualify as forever friends. They had rarely left each other's side since primary school.

Christine was a daughter of a politician/car-business owner in town, while Monica's family was the proprietor of a cargo and shipping business in Mombasa.

Sophia had a dimpled smile as they walked away, happy that the two ladies, who had scared her on arrival, had, over the evening, improved their manners to the extent that she could make little space for them in her guarded circle of friends.

After dinner Richie and Sophia drove back home. He parked in front of his parents' house, held her hand to his mouth and kissed each of her knuckles. "What are your plans for our tomorrow?"

"I see that your ten-day travel made you lose count of days. Tomorrow is Friday, a workday."

"Still working? I assumed you had resigned when I found you asleep at four o'clock, on a workday."

"I have told you before that I will not resign. I will take leave when the time is right, maybe in December." She leaned her head on Richie's shoulder. "I have missed you all these days. Stop asking me about work and resignations."

Her mention of taking leave in December dampened the happiness Richie had built all evening. Not wanting to let her see how hurt he was, he got out of the car and opened the door for her. He walked her to the door and let her into the house before he returned and drove the car to the garage, at a speed his father would discourage on the spot.

As the Mwasimba sons came of age and learned to drive, driving at high speed was one of the topics their father brought up at their weekly family meetings.

Whenever he was home and heard a speeding car within the compound, Mwasimba would sermon the driver, be it one of his sons or their friends, for an uninterrupted lengthy talk on the dangers of driving at high speed.

Richie parked the car and stayed inside, reflective. He pondered how to convince Sophia that it would not be proper for her and for the company if she appeared tired while at work. With both elbows on the steering wheel, he supported his head between his hands, thoughtful.

After about five minutes, he instinctively checked the driving mirror and saw one of the night security guards walk towards the car.

Richie got out of the car, banged the door shut and walked towards the house.

The guard stopped, responded to a greeting from Richie before he turned and walked back to the gate.

Richie strolled towards the house, with two of the family dogs by his side. He comforted himself that whatever the situation, Sophia was still the love of his life. He could not even try to imagine a life without her or a life where she had to struggle for anything, including working so hard for money.

By the time he was inside the house, he had decided that he would go to work the next day.

Chapter 19

Richie woke up in a happy mood. He got out of bed, turned back and kissed Sophia on the forehead before going to the bathroom.

He whistled a country music love song, only pausing to brush his teeth. He whistled more songs as he showered, and only stopped when he walked into the bedroom.

He turned to the dresser mirror and held the collar of his white shirt one more time, straightened it well with the blue floral necktie. He smoothed a hand down his Armani navy-blue coat and trousers.

Richie took shoeless strides to the bed, lifted Sophia's hand, and kissed her fingers, an action which woke her up. He kissed her again and wished her a good day before he walked out of the bedroom.

Sophia looked at her bedside clock and saw that she had four more minutes before her 6:45am alarm went off.

She pulled a bed sheet over her head and tried to sleep as she heard the alarm go off. She stretched her hand, silenced it, and placed it on Richie's side of the bed. Her reasoning was that the soft pillow would reduce the intensity of the next ring, and she would not need to stretch far to switch it off.

A soft knock on the bedroom door startled her out of sleep. Before she could ask who was at the door, her eyes fell on the clock beside her, she stared at the short arm on eight and the long one on four, 8:20am.

The clock dropped to the floor as she lifted both feet out of bed, instead of her usual slow motion of one leg at a time. "I am a bit late but will be ready soon," she called out in a raised voice as she hurried to the bathroom.

Within thirty minutes, she had showered and dressed in office attire. As she approached the dining room, she was not pleased to see Patience eating breakfast.

"Good morning Mum," Sophia greeted as she pulled a chair and sat. "I stayed in bed longer, that way I can extend my day at the office." She explained without being asked.

Patience held the teacup which she had lifted halfway to her mouth. "Today is Friday. You could choose to go back to bed after breakfast."

Sophia did not look up from the glass in her hand. She responded while serving a cocktail of mango, orange, and pineapple juice. "I need to be at the office, Friday is the day I normally plan for the coming week." She lifted the glass of juice to her mouth.

Patience watched Sophia's throat rise and fall to the rhythm of juice gulping down into her empty stomach.

When the glass was empty, she heaved herself out of the chair. "Thanks for the packed lunch," she said, as she lifted the lunch bag from the far end of the dining table. "I will eat this when I arrive at the office."

Patience's eyes trailed her as Sophia picked up her handbag and walked out through the kitchen door.

Patience refilled her cup and stared at it until it became cold. She was thoughtful, questioned what it was that was forcing Sophia to report to work, even on a day when her body was not willing. If it was money, Richie had enough for both. If they ran out of money, Mwasimba would loan them millions until they were either able to repay or keep it as a gift.

She shook her head, as she recalled that for five months now, the Amex card registered in Sophia's name had been attracting a monthly bill of 0:00 shillings. She made a mental note to ask Richie or Sophia why the card was not in use.

She pulled the teacup that Sophia had not used and filled it with hot tea, took two sips before placing it on the coaster. She was reflective, If Sophia and Richie were low on money, she would encourage them to stay in the north wing until they were financially comfortable before moving out, or they could stay on and not think of moving out at all. The house had three wings with many empty bedrooms - more than enough space for two families.

As Patience held onto the dining table to stand up, the house phone rang. She hurried and picked it up, fearing Sophia could be unwell and was calling for help.

"Good morning, Mum. How's your morning?" Richie asked, making Patience more worried. She imagined Sophia could be unwell somewhere along the road and had called Richie. To Patience, Richie must be calling her, because if Sophia needed help, she must be closer to home than the office, for she had not left too long ago.

She pressed the phone receiver closer to her ear, waiting for Richie to say something. When he did not, she spoke. "Sophia overslept a bit. She will be there soon. She left the house a few minutes ago."

"Thanks Mum. I thought she would stay home today. Bye, Mum," Richie said before he ended the call and walked towards Michael's office.

~~~~~~~

Earlier that morning, Richie had called Michael and asked for an appointment to discuss a not-so-personal, not-so-official issue.

After waiting for Richie to elaborate and no further details were forthcoming, Michael had asked him to come over at 9:00am.

Richie's plan was to ask Michael to release Sophia from work. On the way to Michael's office, Richie had stopped by Sophia's office to greet her. However, she was not in and her office door was locked, though she had insisted the night before that she would go to work the next day.
~~~~~~~

Before reaching Michael's office, he had stopped along the corridor and telephoned their home number where his mother answered the call.

Richie knocked and entered Michael's office. "Is it okay if we talk from the restaurant or Nick's place?"

Nick, their youngest brother resided at the topmost floor of Akoth Towers, the same house Richie had occupied until he married. Nick lived there from Monday to Friday for easy travel to and from school.

When Richie entered the office, Michael could tell there was something bothering him. The first thought was an emergency, especially considering that it was past nine and Sophia had not yet arrived at the office.

Michael stared at Richie without uttering a word. He shut the screen of his computer and stood up. "I will be okay with your choice." He walked to the front of his desk and looked at Richie.

Richie walked towards the office door, which meant they were going downstairs to the restaurant.

As they walked towards the elevator, Michael relaxed, convincing himself there was no emergency, as Richie would have voiced it by now. "How was your evening? Did you manage to have a rest?"

"Busy but good. Sophia and I went out for tea and dinner, which meant we slept rather late, but well."

"Sounds like you had fun after being apart for so many days," Michael said as the elevator chimed, and the two doors parted.

They stepped inside at the same time. Richie pressed second floor. "I will work on my travel report today. We can discuss the next steps on Monday."

Michael was now fully relaxed as he listened to Richie talk of his plans for the day and for the coming week.

The brothers entered the restaurant which was almost empty. Being just after nine in the morning, most employees were busy on their second hour of the day's work.

They chose a corner table, farthest from the cashier's counter.

Michael called out to a waiter who was nearby. "Good morning. Today, there was no breakfast at Mwasimba house. Bring some hot tea for the boys."

Each pulled a chair and sat.

Michael sat on a chair facing the expansive restaurant floor while Richie sat in the opposite chair, facing the wall behind Michael.

Richie sat with both hands on the table encircling his cup. He spoke without looking up. "I need some advice from you, more as a brother and less as Sophia's Director."

"Hi. I'm Director of everyone," Michael said, trying to lighten the tension that he felt in Richie's voice.

Ignoring the comment, Richie continued. "I know our talk might end up on you as the Director, but for now, it's just brotherly advice."

Michael sipped tea and placed his cup on the table. "I am listening. No problem can be too big if everyone is fine, health-wise."

"There is no problem, though the issue touches a bit on health, Sophia's health."

Michael extended his left hand and touched Richie's. "I hope she is okay."

"She is. I notice that she is getting tired by the day. Will it be okay if she took early leave from work or even work half day…, perhaps just a few hours a day?"

"Sophia has been a hardworking PA since her first day of work…," Michael said.

Richie's eyebrows pulled in, fearing that Michael was not willing to release Sophia from the office until her delivery date neared.

Michael, on the other hand, had paused, on remembering how Sophia got the job as his PA, a job earmarked for an applicant with an internal recommendation.

On the morning of the interviews, Michael was convinced that Elvis, his driver, had hit the girl crossing the road to board a matatu, a public transport vehicle waiting across the road.

Elvis had gone ahead to the office to drop Michael before he could visit a police station to record a statement.

When Michael recognized Sophia as the third interviewee for the day, he gave her the job, partly in gratitude that she was fine and uninjured after the way she had rolled to the other side of the road in front of a waiting matatu. "Sophia has made my work-life very manageable. I will let her take leave whenever she decides, ask her to fill the necessary forms today."

Richie smiled, a nervous smile with only his left cheek rising upwards. "That is where I need your help."

Michael lifted his cup towards his mouth but stopped halfway. His attention was drawn to the entrance to the restaurant. He put the cup back on the table as his lips twisted into a lopsided smile. He waved good morning.

Richie turned to see who Michael was greeting. He glanced and quickly repositioned his head back to the table and stared into his tea. He lifted the cup and took his first sip of tea as he heard Michael say. "She left? I thought she was looking for me."

"I doubt. I saw she had her lunch bag, which means she had come to eat."

Richie took another sip from his cup.

Michael looked up and saw that the staff of the restaurant were staring towards their table, maybe formulating their version of a story, why the two brothers were at the restaurant unusually early, and Richie's pregnant wife had walked in, and out quickly.

"Did you chase my sister away?" Michael asked the restaurant staff.

The oldest of the three waiters responded. "I am sad that you scared away my daughter."

There was loud laughter as Michael turned back to Richie. "You were explaining something before."

"I love Sophia and would like her to take leave and stay at home. She deserves to rest, sleep more and wake up only when necessary."

Michael noted that Richie was getting emotional. Fearing that the restaurant staff could still be curious, he pulled a cell phone from his breast pocket and stood up. Richie looked up, as Michael said. "Let's go upstairs."

Richie emptied his cup and stood up. As they walked out, he forced a smile at the waiters as he pointed to Michael. "Double the bill and put it under his account."

They quickened their steps out as the restaurant, as the staff laughed.

Michael was busy on his phone as they rode in the elevator to the 52nd floor.

Richie stood at one corner of the elevator, a bit too far from his brother. Thoughts flipped through Richie's mind. He wondered if Michael had found their discussion useless and was going back to his office to continue with his day's tasks. Or had Michael decided that they continue with the conversation from his office? That option would not be good, as Sophia might come to Michael's office, disrupting their discussion.

The elevator chimed 52nd floor, doors opened, and they stepped out. Michael called someone on the phone and talked. Richie walked by his side.

They waved to Liz at the reception desk and walked on.

Michael unlocked his office door, and Richie followed inside.

Instead of turning right to his desk, Michael turned left and walked to the internal elevator hidden behind a floor-to-roof bookcase.

He completed the phone call as the elevator door closed, and they were hauled upwards.

"I remembered Justus is not on duty today. Let's go to Nick's hideout," Michael explained as the elevator doors opened and they walked out.

Michael punched the code to access the front door, they walked inside and sat on high stools by the kitchen island. Shortly, Michael descended from his stool, went to the fridge where he opened and closed the door. He opened a nearby cabinet, grabbed two water glasses, and filled them from the fridge water dispenser. He placed one glass in front of Richie. "Yes, she is free to fill in the paperwork anytime, even today."

Richie extended his left hand and folded his fingers, one-by-one, starting with his pinkie, followed by the ring finger. "I can count beyond all my fingers." He made eye contact with Michael. "The number of times I have tried to convince her - from home to Naivasha, to the clubs, in the bedroom, the compound, to last night, without success." He completed the sentence as he sprung down from the stool and walked towards the corridor to the four bedrooms.

Michael could tell from the slanted shoulders that his younger brother was hurting. That morning he was not the same man who always walked with boxed shoulders, like he lived in a gym, lifting weights. Michael reflected on what he had just learned - Richie had tried many times to get Sophia to take leave, all in vain.

A smile appeared on his face as he thought of how different people could be. From Beauta, his wife, who had made it clear that she would only seek employment if she ran out of more interesting things in life. To Sophia, his sister-in-law who craved to work until the hospital labour ward beckoned her.

Richie walked in. As he climbed upon the stool, Michael asked, "What have you decided, to wait and count your toes before giving up?"

Richie made himself comfortable and took a sip from his glass of water. "What if you share the tactics you used on Beauta?"

Michael laughed aloud. Laughter that would have easily vibrated the kitchen windows were it not that they were far, at least twenty feet away from where the two sat. "That was none of my making, just sheer luck on my side, if I can call it that for now."

"Does that mean I am consulting with the wrong man?"

"Could be.... My suggestion is that you keep trying. If I tried, Sophia might construe it to mean that I do not want her to work for me, or to work at the company."

"There won't be a problem with that. My plan is that she stays home while I work and provide for all our financial needs."

"People come from different families, for now you can only persist until she gives in. When are you guys due?"

Richie laughed. "That'll be your homework, do the math. I was her first and only one." He patted his chest then stepped down from the stool. "Do we go, or I leave you here?"

Michael stepped down and stretched out a hand to Richie. "You're a lucky man. Count me out if she reads your face on what we have been talking about."

"No worries. I will handle everything."

They walked out of the apartment and into the waiting elevator.

On reaching the office, Michael went to his desk, as Richie opened the door and walked out into the corridor.

Richie entered his office with a stride as he needed to focus on writing his travel report. There was a whole weekend ahead for him to worry about what to say to Sophia.

Chapter 20

Richie sat at the dining table long after he finished having breakfast. He served juice then stared into the glass without lifting it to his mouth. He had one wish, that his mother would not arrive for breakfast before Sophia did.

Luckily for him, Sophia arrived, though she abandoned her breakfast when he asked, "Did you write your letter of resignation yet? I talked with Michael about it last week."

She went back into the bedroom while voicing her concerns. "I do not understand why you want me out of a job. Please let me go to work, my source of income."

He followed her. "I am so sorry for spoiling your Monday morning. I could not tell you yesterday, as the whole family was here most of the day. Please understand."

Sophia folded her arms across her chest. "Understand? How do I understand when you are trying to get me out of a job? How will I survive without my salary?"

"Remember the card you have refused to use?"

Sophia tilted her head upwards and their eyes locked. He saw the confusion spread all over her face, so he explained. "The Amex card I gave you many months ago, you are supposed to use it whenever you need money. No need to worry about the payments."

He took one step and closed the gap between them, drew her into a hug and rested his chin on her head. "If you prefer cash, I will bring you a debit card."

She freed herself from his chest and walked on to the bathroom. He hurried, reached her, and cuddled her. He could hear the high heartbeat from her chest, all the way to his chest.

He panicked that her blood pressure might rise, which the doctor had warned would not be good for the baby and mother. He guided her to the two-seater sofa in the bedroom. "I am sorry if I have caused you any anxiety. Please call Michael and let us stay home today."

Sophia wiped tears from her cheeks.

Richie stood up, then went down on one knee in front of her and held her hands to his cheeks, imploring her. "Please, calm down for the sake of your health, your blood pressure, as the doctor warned."

She lifted the sleeve of her jacket and wiped off more tears.

Richie stood up and extended both hands to her. She held on and pulled herself up from the chair. "I am going to the office."

"I am okay with that if it will calm you down, lower your blood pressure. I will leave after you."

Sophia went to the bathroom, cleaned all traces of her tears while reflecting on what had made her angry so early on a Monday morning.

Back in the bedroom, she sat next to Richie, lifted his bent head, held his face between her hands and kissed him on the mouth. "I am fine. I will be okay at work."

Pressing onto his thighs for support, she stood up and walked away, pulling the bedroom door behind her.

After about thirty minutes of reflection, Richie wondered how wise he was to inform Sophia that he had talked with Michael about her need to resign. He wished he had given the idea more thought, or better yet not even mentioned it to her at all.

Without a second thought, he phoned Sophia. She was pleasant, in a happy mood. It was a big relief to him. He reassured her that she could stay at her job for as long as it suited her.

When Sophia said she would consider his offer, he wished her a joyful day and ended the call.

He walked out of the bedroom, greeted his mother in the dining room without stopping, as he would have done on other days. He pushed the library door open, went and logged into his office files and worked on his travel report. When he was satisfied with the details, he emailed a copy to Michael and asked for his feedback.

After an hour, he received a response. "I like the contents of your report, very many possibilities exist out there that we had not thought of before. You may come to my office for a brief discussion."

Richie smiled as he typed a reply. "I am working from home today."

After a moment, he saw his cell phone flash with a message which he assumed was from Sophia until he read it. "Is that your latest agreement? Your wife told me she would apply for leave in December."

Richie read the message again before he put his phone away. He was concerned, that even after he had given Sophia the leeway to decide, she had stuck to her earlier date of December as the time she would go on leave, rather close to her January expected date of delivery.

After lunch, he spent the afternoon on the Internet. He checked information on how the financial markets in the East had performed now that they had closed business for the day. He would check on the European market and then thereafter American markets as they opened for business.

At four o'clock, he sent a message to Sophia. "Hi Sunshine, Mum has been in the house all day. Do you want to go for a walk with her today?"

"No thanks. What about you?"

"I started following global markets from the East, now in Europe. I am waiting to catch the Americas as they wake up."

He waited, but there was no response from her. His hope was that if she agreed to go for a walk with his mother, they might get into a chat on her leave, that way Patience would ask when she planned to start her leave.

His reasoning was that the more the family members showed concern about Sophia persisting to go to work, the easier it would be for her to either take leave or resign.

At some point, Richie thought of going to talk with his mother about it, but changed his mind, deciding it would be better if the discussion was Sophia's initiative.

He spent the rest of the evening in the library, though he achieved little with the task of following the global financial markets. He was preoccupied with Sophia's reluctance regarding leave.

Chapter 21

Stella took the seven-hour bus ride to the city after Sophia had turned down Richie's offer for a company vehicle to drive her to the city. Sophia's argument was that her mother would be more comfortable on the bus than sitting alone in a big car, being driven from her rural home to the city.

Richie would have challenged her decision on travel, but he chose not to. He had a more pressing issue to deal with—securing Sophia's leave from work.

As the weekend approached, Sophia and Richie were excited, but for very different reasons. She would be seeing her mother soon, while Richie was hopeful that his mother-in-law would advise Sophia to start an early maternity leave.

Sophia would have liked to visit her mother at Joy's house on Friday evening, but she was very tired after working all day to clear her office chores for Friday and Monday. She took Monday off to be with her mother before her travel back to the village scheduled for Tuesday.

"You look tired. Is everything okay?" Richie asked when Sophia arrived home after work.

She chose not to respond. Instead, she went and sat in the family room.

Richie followed her and did not need her response to conclude that all was not well. Unlike the other days when her arrival from work followed a predictable routine of changing from office clothes, drinking tea before taking a walk, she did not follow it on that day.

"I will skip the evening walk. One day will not make much difference." Sophia said as she smoothed her bulging belly.

Richie, who had sat on the opposite sofa, looked at her. "It will be better to take a proper rest today, that way you will have enough energy when Mama comes in tomorrow. Lest she thinks we are overworking you."

Her face brightened. "Nothing will bring joy to Mama like seeing her daughter carry on with normal tasks, going to the office until the day before the baby arrives."

Richie jerked to standing position before he sat down again. "That was a joke shared only between us. No woman should do that, work to the last day, especially if she loves the baby she has been entrusted to carry."

Sophia looked at Richie as she pressed on the right side of her stomach with three of her fingers. "The baby is fine, kicking like I am a football or netball field."

Richie crossed over and sat next to her as she said, "I need to go lay down for some minutes."

He helped her to her feet and followed her into the bedroom where she picked a nightie and went to the bathroom. Richie stared as she took short steps until she was out of his sight.

Ten minutes later, she returned, having showered and changed. She sat on the bed, lifted one leg at a time onto the bed and lay in sleeping position.

Richie went to her side, pulled the sheets and duvet up to her neck and kissed her on the forehead. "Six o'clock seems too early to retire to bed. I will wake you up to eat dinner." He walked out of the bedroom.

Though tired, Sophia did not drift into sleep immediately. Her mind was busy, reflective. She worried about whether she had worked too hard for her six-month pregnancy. She worried what to tell her mother if she still looked haggard the next day. Would her mother ask her to visit a doctor, or worse, ask her to take leave from work?

On further thought, she consoled herself. Her mother would not think of leave, when she herself rarely took a break from her normal routine before and after the delivery of her six children.

The widespread practice in the village was that women engaged in household chores until the day of their delivery, unless there was a complication with a pregnancy. Sophia recalled that even women carrying twins rarely found a need to stop doing daily chores, except in the last one or two months, when a relative came over to help with tasks that required one to bend or involve in heavy lifting.

Sophia was apprehensive on recalling some of the information shared by her doctor. Dr. Rajur had mentioned on more than two occasions, that though pregnancy was a natural life event, women are individuals when it comes to experience.

She worried that she could be within the group of the odd women since she resides in a city and works in an office where she sits most of the day. Would her lifestyle, whereby she is driven to and from the office, and the changes in the food she consumed, make her different from her mother and other women in the village? She wondered whether living in the city was the reason Richie's mother had chosen to stay home while Mwasimba went to work.

~~~~~~

Richie went to the family room in the east wing of the house where the visitors' bedrooms were situated. He called and talked with Michael briefly, asking if Sophia had put in her leave application.

"What if you ask her? Sometimes my employees send their applications to human resources first, and only inform me after the application is approved."

Richie felt defeated. Supporting his forehead on his left hand, he said, "She came home very tired and is asleep. I will ask her when she wakes up."

After a long moment of silence, Michael said. "Make time. Discuss the issue with her."
~~~~~~

"I have done that uncountable times, including today. I do not know what to do next."

"I hear you. Talking could mean something else, like being open-minded and exploring the different options together."

Richie did not say what was in his mind. He had wanted to tell Michael that he was the most open-minded man. He let Sophia stay in employment even when that was not the practice in their family. He would have wanted to add that he had given Sophia an Amex card that she had so far not used at all, and he was willing to buy a house just as she had asked.

Richie ended the call without saying bye to Michael. He realized his folly and typed a message. "Sorry. I was not being rude. I got lost in thought and disconnected our call involuntarily."

"Understandable. It's good that you are focusing all your thoughts into the issue. Regards and see you tomorrow afternoon."

Richie smiled as he read the message from Michael before he tossed the phone on a nearby coffee table, where it landed with a thud.

He was thinking about what options he had not explored with Sophia. He picked up the phone and called Enock. The phone rang three times before Enock answered.

Richie thundered into the phone. "Is my position at the bank still open or have you given it to a potential girlfriend?"

"I am still waiting for you to make both of us winners."

Richie laughed. "I have my doubts if she will accept that position, which means you lose." He chuckled. "Anyway, here is an easier assignment for you." He paused before completing the sentence. "I will be at your desk tomorrow morning to –."

Enock interrupted. "Come in before eleven. I have a meeting from midday, unless you want us to meet after work."

"What I need is expedited service, not your two-day wait time." He paused and only continued when Enock did not talk. "What I need is for you to add my wife to my account and issue her a debit card."

"The normal items, her photos and signature," Enock said, like he was out of breath.

Richie chuckled. "My account does not require photos."

"Yes, Sir. I had no idea you were adding her to your main account." Enock faked a cough before he continued. "Come over tomorrow and sign out the card. We already have the signature she gave for the credit card."

There was silence on the line as Richie juggled words in his head, how to respond to the use of yes sir by Enock. "I now see why you need a wife, soon," Richie said.

Enock chuckled. "I am still waiting for the girl you promised me."

"Having an adorable wife like mine means we are one. We share everything, including that account." He chuckled, "And many other items that the phone will not allow me to utter."

Richie moved the phone further away from his ear as Enock responded with loud laughter. "I have changed my mind. Come in at midday. That way we can have the Saturday afternoon together. I must hear of the part that the phone cannot transmit."

"Sorry. You will have to wait until next weekend. My mother-in-law will visit tomorrow, so I will come in as the doors to the bank swing open, and dash back home to welcome her."

"Is Sophia there with you? Please may I greet her?"

"No. If you want to talk with her, come for tea on Sunday. We will be home."

"See you then. Bye bro," Enock concluded their telephone conversation.

Chapter 22

Monday morning, Sophia forced herself out of bed. Her plan was to spend the day with her mother before she traveled back to the village the next day.

Sophia needed to chat with her in private, ask her questions about pregnancy, birth, and motherhood.

Though she had been with her mother on Saturday when she visited the Mwasimba home, they had not had any private moment. Many family members had turned up to welcome her.

Being a believer in the theory of ups and downs in life, Sophia convinced herself Monday would be an 'up'. Saturday, when her mother visited had also been an 'up'. Sunday afternoon was a 'down' when Enock tried to talk her into resigning from her job. So, Monday should be an 'up'.

Sophia arrived at Joy's apartment at eight thirty in the morning. The driver walked with her to the third floor of the apartment building and rang the doorbell.

Stella opened the door. "My child, welcome. You must have woken up exceedingly early."

Sophia entered the living room and strode around, like she was inspecting the place.

Stella tried to convince the driver to get into the house, but he objected, explained that he was going to the office for another assignment.

Sophia went back to the door and thanked him for seeing her safely to the house.

Stella closed the front door and turned to hear the monologue Sophia was having with a framed work of art on the wall. "Hard to miss that a designer lives in this house. I was here a few weeks ago, and now I see that the place has changed, again," Sophia said as she walked into the dining room and inspected a side table holding another framed work of art.

Stella stood in the living room and watched until Sophia joined her.

"Thank you for welcoming me on Saturday. You are with a good family, they were available to welcome me." Stella had a broad smile as she aligned the coffee table into its usual position in the living room.

She turned to Sophia. "Did you say the two sons and their wives traveled from their houses?" She asked as she walked into the kitchen and returned with a food tray. "Come we eat breakfast."

"Mama, I ate breakfast not long ago, but I will sit with you while you eat." Sophia followed her mother into the dining room.

"Come, come. You must have woken up early to eat and arrive here this early considering how everyone talks of the heavy traffic in the city as people travel to and from work."

"Ooh Mama. Nothing close to what you're thinking about. There is a chef in the house, someone employed to cook, though our Mum is always in the kitchen helping. We wake up and find breakfast on the table, whenever one is ready to eat."

"So, when do you get to cook for your husband?"

Sophia tilted her head upwards, towards the ceiling as she tapped her pointer finger on her cheek. "On a few occasions, Mum allows me to assist her with small tasks such as to pass to her ingredients or stirring the food she is cooking. That is how we live."

Sophia guessed that her mother would be astonished that there are households which employ people just to cook for others, as done in restaurants and hotels?

Stella served tea into two cups, and mandazi in two side plates. She placed one in front of Sophia. "If I remember well from my time of carrying babies, you will be hungry soon. You may as well have another breakfast."

Mother and daughter ate while they conversed on a variety of subjects. By the time they vacated the dining room and went to the kitchen to prepare lunch, Stella had updated Sophia on everyone at home and in the village.

Her younger brothers - Babu, Charlie, and Kevin were working hard in their studies. Thanks to Sophia providing money for school fees, Kevin who was now in his final year of school, had not been sent home for school fees like before.

Sophia was happy to learn that Mariko, her father had expanded his grocery store into a larger building. He now owned a grocery and wholesale store and had plans to build a brick house for his family.

Mariko sold regular items such as cooking oil, salt, sugar, and matchboxes. Other grocery store owners in the village bought items from him in bulk, instead of traveling the fifteen kilometers to town for the same.

Stella informed Sophia that they had employed a worker to help on the family farm, subsequently releasing Stella to focus more on the homestead and her vegetable garden.

After lunch, Sophia excused herself and headed to Joy's bedroom for a nap.

Stella found Sophia's need for a nap strange. "Girls of today, do you work a full day, or do you go home to rest after lunch?" she inquired as she washed the dishes.

"Mama, I still work full time. My body seems to know when I am in the office and when I am home. I will take advantage of being home today," She left the kitchen.

"Has your new family not asked you to stay home, as the rich usually do?"

"Who would pay school fees if I stopped working?" Sophia asked, sounding agitated.

Stella turned off the tap and walked out of the kitchen. "Joy. She told me she now has a well-paying job. Give her something to do, or she will spend all her money on clothes and shoes for herself." Stella wiped her wet hands on the apron. "Did I not hear you ask how she's always buying things, that the house looks different each time you visit?"

"She will start paying fees next year when Kevin goes to university," Sophia said as she walked to the bedroom.

Stella returned to the kitchen.

~~~~~~~

There were voices coming from somewhere in the house. Sophia lifted her head, supported it on one elbow, trying to remember where she was.

After she squeezed sleep out of her eyes twice, she saw some familiar items ..., she was in Joy's room. She lifted one leg, followed by the other and stepped on the carpet. She heaved her body into a standing position and walked into the bathroom where she washed her face and used the toilet.

Sophia stepped into the living room.

Richie walked towards her as she entered the dining room. He squeezed her hand fondly. "Did we wake you up? Mama tells me you went to sleep after lunch." He pulled out a dining chair for her.

Sophia yawned as she sat down. "I took advantage of my day off from work to sleep." She turned to Stella who was serving tea into a cup. "Thanks, Mama. Tea is what I need now." She picked up the cup her mother had filled and placed it right in front of her.
~~~~~~~

She made eye contact with Richie who had been staring at her. From his facial expression, she guessed he had a lot of questions for her.

"Maybe Mama can convince you that you need to take leave and stay home." Richie said.

"I will get bored staying home and doing nothing." She turned at Stella. "Going to work helps me count the remaining days faster."

"Remember, you and Mum can go to the mall to shop for whatever you like, another way to pass the time," Richie said as he picked a mandazi before turning to Stella. "Tomorrow, Sophia can take you to the mall for your shopping."

Holding a cup next to her mouth, Stella said, "Tomorrow, I will be on the bus going home."

"Before you see more of this city? Please extend your stay for another two days. Sophia will be excited to walk the malls with her two mothers, a rare opportunity."

Stella refilled her cup with tea. "I might consider your suggestion, to stay."

"Mama, I had only today off. I will be back to the office tomorrow." After a short pause, Sophia added, "But we can go to shops in the city from three o'clock. I will ask Silas to come with you, though you should be able to take a matatu on your own and call me once you are in the city center. Ask the matatu to drop you off near Akoth Towers, everyone knows the building."

Richie released a breath he had been holding. He worried how his pregnant wife was going to walk in and out of shops in the busy city streets. "I have a different suggestion. Sophia can leave the office after lunch, come here and pick you up to go to the mall for the shopping."

He turned to Sophia seated on his left side. "It might be difficult to walk in and out of shops in the city center. You will get more tired. Better to shop at the mall. Please remember to carry your cards for payment."

Sophia stretched her hand under the table and placed it on Richie's lap. "I have money to pay for the items, and—"

The opening of the front door to the house interrupted her sentence. Joy and Silas walked into the house.

"Welcome and thanks for staying with Mama while I was away earning money," Joy said as she reached the dining room. She hugged Sophia then patted Richie on the shoulder.

Richie and Sophia acknowledged a salute from Silas before Sophia addressed Joy. "Bring the money to big sister. How was your day at work?"

Joy washed hands at the sink, pulled a chair and sat down.

Stella walked to the kitchen and returned with a tea flask and two cups.

With her hands clasped together, Joy turned to Sophia. "My money would feel like coins in your hand. What with the money of the two of you together?" she pointed from Sophia to Richie. "I see double money." She laughed aloud while she picked one of the two cups that Stella had filled with tea.

"You are very right," Richie said to Joy. Before you opened the door, I was telling Sophia to take Mama to the mall to shop before she travels back home."

Stella stood up and picked her cup. "I need to check on the vegetables cooking in the kitchen. Let me know if you need more tea." She walked away.

Holding a cup near her mouth, Joy looked at Sophia. "I will take an unpaid day off tomorrow and come with you to the mall." She shifted her eyes to Richie. "I will hide a few of my items on Mama's list." She smiled, "Nothing big enough to dent the Mwasimba's account."

Richie laughed. "Your items will be paid for if you help them select a suit for my father-in-law, complete with a shirt and necktie. Thanks, Joy." He kissed Sophia on the cheek. "Deal sealed."

As Silas laughed, Sophia turned to Joy without any trace of the dimples on her cheeks. "The reason you cannot come with us," she admonished Joy.

"What will I do in the house since I have already taken a day off, in my mind?"

Joy had a natural eye for fashion long before she studied design at the university. When Sophia started working as PA at the Mwasimba Group of Companies, Joy made it her duty to select and combine clothing items for Sophia, from the second-hand clothes they traded in. The carefully selected and well-coordinated outfits had helped Sophia gain respect as a well-dressed PA.

Joy's volunteering to go shopping with them was a big relief to Richie. It meant she would convince Sophia and Stella to visit the mall instead of shops in the city center. He was certain Joy would also alert him in case Sophia became very tired, and he would gladly go drive Sophia home.

That evening Richie was happy as he drove Sophia home. One, he had managed to get her to agree to work a half-day the next day, and two, he was almost certain that pairing up with Joy, Sophia would use the Amex card she had been carrying without ever using even once. If she preferred to use cash, she had the debit card he had given her on Saturday morning.

He also knew that the next time he asked Sophia to start shopping for the baby, Joy would be ready and willing to accompany her.

Chapter 23

On arrival home, Richie and Sophia went for a walk. As they walked around the compound, Sophia said, "I have been thinking about tomorrow, I will ask Joy not to miss work just because of shopping, I can do it with Mama as earlier planned."

"It is not like Joy will be asking for an afternoon off every week."

"You don't understand that Joy needs to work all her hours. Anyway, I will talk with her and hear what she has to say."

Richie squeezed her hand as they stepped back into the house. They sat in the family room to watch TV, though each was deep in thought.

Sophia reflected on her events of the day and wondered how she agreed to let her mother change her travel plans. Joy had bought gifts for everyone at home, so her mother was good to travel the next day, Tuesday.

The other thing that worried Sophia was that if Joy came along for the shopping trip, she would pick many items for Stella, sending the wrong message to their parents. Sophia did not want her parents to think that she could afford to buy them whatever they wanted.

She also had a strong feeling that Joy would pick designer items that cost more than similar items from regular shops in the city center. She juggled strategies in her head about how to dissuade Joy from joining them on the shopping expedition the next day.

Richie absently intertwined and disentangled their fingers. He was reflective, wondering how to explain to Sophia that if she was worried about money, there was no way she would ever see the bill after scanning the Amex card or paying with the debit card.

The practice within the Mwasimba family was that credit card bills of each family member went to the family accountant. The accountant verified that there were no inadmissible expenses before he passed the bills for payment.

The muscles on Richie's face relaxed on recalling that all Sophia's costs, including Joy's designer items, would qualify for payment. It would be the first time the card would have a bill after half a year.

Rather spontaneously, he asked. "Have you considered your resignation, now that you slept after lunch again?"

Sophia leaned and rested her head on his chest. "I slept because I had the day off, not because I was tired."

"My better sense tells me you slept because you could not help it. Please take leave. You deserve to rest adequately."

"I made a promise to you that I will take leave once my body needs it, and as of now, I am very fine." She picked up the remote and changed the TV channel to the money markets.

"By insisting on going to work, you make me feel like you are working two jobs while I work one. Not fair to you."

Sophia smiled. "I thought you too work two jobs, as a manager and a soon-to-be, director of the new department. If you work two jobs, I too can."

Richie smiled, more from the comparison than their argument. He cuddled and kissed her. "Whatever you say, always know that I love you. You are the best thing that ever happened in my life, and always will be."

She kissed him ack. "Then, let me go to work."

"No." He said in a tone higher than he intended to. He lowered his voice. "Because I love you and would not want to see you struggle this much. Let me handle the struggle for the both of us. Allow me."

Sophia smoothed her stomach. She looked up and locked eyes with Richie then looked away. She was surprised to see that Richie was looking at her instead of at the TV. She had switched to the money markets channel to distract him.

She recalled how it used to be before they got married. She had learned that the one way to distract Richie was by bringing up a discussion on the topic of money and markets. A topic she knew he would engage in without minding the passage of time.

She was surprised that this time he had not focused on the TV even when the program anchor listed earnings of some global businesses, as well as a list of the ones that had made losses in the Asian market.

Sophia covered her face with her left hand, like there was glare from the TV screen.

The next time she came to, Richie was who had been supporting her body while she slept, was waking her up to go for dinner.

She panicked, that perhaps Richie was right about her need to stay home and get a better rest, since she seemed to tire and fall asleep rather easily.

When she lifted her head from his chest, he stretched his left arm outwards and wiggled his fingers, to ease out the numbness he felt.

Once Richie had realized that Sophia had fallen asleep on his chest, he tried ridiculously hard not to make any movement that could wake her from sleep. He thus stayed still for her sake, the reason, after seventy minutes, his left arm felt like it did not belong to his body.

He was glad she had allowed her body to respond to sleep but was also worried that she could be falling asleep in the office without knowing or acknowledging it.

As they walked into the dining room to join his parents and Nick for dinner, Richie made a mental note to ask Michael if Sophia ever fell asleep while in the office.

After Nick finished saying grace and silverware started clicking on dinner plates, Richie took a long look at Nick, prompting Nick to tilt his head upwards. He stared at the ceiling. "Are you wondering why I am home on a Monday? I missed Sophia. I came to greet them." Nick said without looking at Richie.

Everyone at the table laughed.

"I thought you ran away from school, rather, from the house that gets you to school within minutes." Richie replaced his fork on the plate. "Why come home from where it will take you one hour to get to school?"

Patience looked at Richie. "Nick will leave with his dad early in the morning. That will get him to school earlier than usual."

With a grin, Mwasimba glanced from Richie to Nick. He swallowed the food in his mouth before he addressed Patience. "Did I hear you offer the young man a ride in my car?" He chuckled. "Now it's my car, after the boys took over my house in town?"

"Dad, that house is for single, suffering boys like Nick, the reason I vacated it very fast, to be here with Sophia." Richie said.

Sophia winked at Richie. He did not say much after that.

After dinner, Nick and Richie excused themselves and went into the home library while Sophia went to the bedroom.

Richie's hope was that since Sophia had slept after lunch and that evening, she would stay awake to ponder his request. If she did not decide soon about taking leave, he would consult with Dr. Rajur and request him to prescribe for her a medical leave.

Chapter 24

They entered the doctor's consultation room at three-thirty in the afternoon. But by four, Richie could not recall what Dr. Rajur had been talking about. He was deep in thought, weighing the proper words to use to ask the doctor for Sophia could start her maternity leave.

As the doctor stood to see them off to the door, Richie turned to Sophia. "Doctor, is it okay if she can stay home, stop going to work?"

Throughout his thirty-five plus years of practice as a gynecologist, Dr. Rajur had seen enough pregnant women and petrified husbands, including Richie's mother and father. Over the years, the doctor could tell whenever a couple had unresolved issues, especially when a husband was hesitant with their words, or was slow to leave his office.

"Please be seated." Dr. Rajur motioned them back to their chairs as he looked from Sophia to Richie.

Many a time, the doctor had seen men struggle for the right words to ask for a medical leave for their wives. He walked back to his side of the desk, sat down, and pulled his hanging glasses back to the ridge of his nose.

He addressed Sophia. "Is there a concern you forgot to mention?"

Looking down at her fingernails, she turned her eyes to Richie when she heard him say, "She tires very easily during the day. I thought it well if she stays home to have a proper rest."

Sophia wiggled her back against the chair. "I am not sick. I just feel tired occasionally, which is normal. Is it not Doctor?"

Dr. Rajur looked at Richie and back to Sophia. He picked up the receiver on his desk, pressed a button and spoke into the phone, "My apologies to the next patient. I will see them in the next ten minutes, or sooner."

He replaced the receiver on the phone and turned to Sophia. "How do you normally feel before you fall asleep during the day?"

Sophia explained she only felt very tired after consuming a full lunch, which only happened when she was home. She said she was not sick. The baby kicked at certain intervals, and she was usually back to her normal self, alert, within one or two hours.

Dr. Rajur looked at Richie while addressing Sophia. "People are different, especially the expectant women that I see every day. If the tiredness bothers you, let me know so that we revisit your nutrition, though from the last scans, the baby is growing well, which means you are eating well and staying physically active."

Sophia smiled.

Richie's eyebrows pulled close together. "Doctor, I am okay with her staying at home, but she might agree more if you advise her on the same."

Dr. Rajur picked up a pen from a nearby penholder. He twisted the top of the pen on and off while he waited for Sophia or Richie to say something.

When neither of them spoke, Dr. Rajur said, "What I normally do is recommend a medical leave if the patient tells me how they feel, that they are not able to report to work. Otherwise, I have no other way to justify a sick-off."

He looked at Richie. "The only advice I would give is that you go home and discuss the issue. Come back if there is a medical concern, or an agreed upon reason."

"Thanks, doctor. We will do exactly that," Richie said as he stood up and extended a hand to support Sophia to her feet. He held her by the small of her back as they left the room while thanking the doctor again.

Richie and Sophia were driven to a café at the nearby shopping center. Richie's plan, though he did not mention it, was that they would drink tea, thus give Sophia time to rethink her argument. His hope was that she would then ask that they go back to the doctor and request a medical leave based on her frequent need for sleep.

A waiter arrived and handed a menu to each while asking what they would like to drink.

"Thanks. I do not want to eat. I want to go home." Sophia said.

Richie dropped the menu on the table and excused themselves before they walked out of the restaurant.

~~~~~~~

They arrived home and Richie encouraged Sophia to take a nap. He had seen her doze on and off on their drive home.

She agreed.

Richie sat in the family room and switched on the TV though he could not tell what channel was playing. He was thoughtful, reflecting on the various instances he had tried to convince Sophia to resign from work.

He recalled her reaction the first time he had mentioned the company rule which stipulated that if two company staff married, one of them needed to resign from the company.

Richie had assumed that after their wedding Sophia would voluntarily resign from her post. He was surprised when she instead asked why her and not him?

Richie had no words to explain that his managerial position paid more, a salary that could comfortably cater for their financial needs. Even if both had been on a similar pay, he would have liked to explain to Sophia that there was no way he would stop working for his family firm. No other company would give him a job, they would be suspicious on why he had left his father's company.

He thought of the time he explained to Sophia that since she had worked for the company for more than two years, she would receive a good sum of money upon her resignation.
~~~~~~~

She had countered his argument, explaining that money was not her only motivation for being in employment.

A smile appeared on Richie's face upon remembering how he had even promised to give Sophia a monthly income equivalent to seventy percent of her salary if she stayed home. Her response had been that the money would be the same that Richie needed to support the family. There would be no difference.

Richie tried ridiculously hard to recall what strategy he had not used. He had found her a job at a nearby bank, but she had turned down the managerial position. He had talked with Michael whose response was that Sophia could take leave whenever she wanted to, but he would not ask her to resign.

Richie recalled that not too long ago, he had asked Sophia to apply for her annual leave days while waiting to take her maternity leave, which she had turned down, saying she planned to combine her annual and maternity leave days to have more time with the baby.

There was a cough, making Richie jerk into an upright position.

"I saw you're in deep thought. I feared you would miss a heartbeat if I interfered," Patience said as she sat on the sofa opposite from Richie.

"We went to the doctor, and Sophia did not ask for medical leave as I had hoped. I have been thinking, wondering how to ask her to stay home." The words escaped from his mouth before he could reconsider them.

"Why, don't you want her to work?"

"I do, and I like her commitment to work. My only concern is the number of times she falls asleep during the day." He glanced at the entrance to the north wing, "Though she says it never happens in the office because she avoids eating a full meal for lunch."

"Does that mean she skips lunch while in the office?"

Richie tilted his neck downwards, like he did not want his Mum to see his pulled in eyebrows. "That is my other worry. I hope she's not denying herself better nutrition for the sake of staying at work."

There was a long stretch of silence.

Richie picked up the remote and changed the television channel from news to the weather channel.

After about five minutes of silence, Patience stood up. "What if you discuss with her, let her come up with a solution? All you will do is to give her your full ear," Patience said before she walked away.

Richie weighed his mother's words as his mood altered between frustration and reflection. He was disappointed that his mother did not wait for him to share the list of strategies he had used, trying to convince Sophia, all in vain.

He got angry. Sophia could not see that there was a problem with her falling asleep in the middle of the day. He walked out of the house, following the route he normally took with Sophia for her evening exercise.

At the orchard, he stopped, plucked a mature apple and bit a large chunk. He looked up at the tree like he was in search of more apples, though there were many hanging low from nearby branches. He was not searching for a fruit, but for a solution to this persisting matter, a way forward.

He reflected on the words from his mother as he took a second bite of the apple. Were it not for the apple filling his mouth, Richie would have voiced aloud the thoughts in his mind, that he would discuss the issue with Sophia, again?

He was pensive, as he walked to the back of the house. At that moment, it dawned on him that in all his earlier attempts to convince Sophia to resign, what he had done was instruct her. He had not asked for her opinion. He threw the remaining apple back to the orchard, scattering birds from the fruit trees.

Richie walked into the house through the kitchen door and did not turn to say anything to his mother in the kitchen.

He tiptoed into the bathroom and took a shower until Sophia opened the bathroom door. "I thought someone had left a tap running, the water has been splashing for a long time."

"I'm washing away my old self," Richie said as he turned the tap off.

"What do you mean by your old self?"

"I went on a walk around the compound and my brains opened up with innovative ideas."

"I see you have showered. Does that mean there'll be no walk for me this evening??" Sophia asked before she walked away. She stopped at the family room and changed the TV channel to news which she watched until Patience walked in. "I saw Richie go for a walk without you, come we go. I need to go for a walk, I have been indoors, doing some office work."

"I might skip today. I hope it will not hurt." Sophia liked her regular evening walk. It helped relax her legs and hands. Her refusal to go for a walk was based on fear. She wondered if Richie had shared with Patience what had transpired while on their visit to the doctor.

What would she say to Patience if she asked her to stop going to work, which she could do in her capacity as her mother-in-law, and a member of the board of the Mwasimba Group of Companies? After a long moment of silence, Patience walked away. "I will be in the kitchen in case you change your mind about the walk."

Chapter 25

During the week preceding the inauguration of the new department, Africa Markets & Money Exchange (AMME), Richie worked for a minimum of twelve hours each day. He left the house at six in the morning and get back just in time to join the family at the dinner table.

His near absence from Sophia's days gave her time to reflect on her personal life as a daughter, sister, wife, employee and soon, mother to be.

On some days when Patience was not home in the evening, Sophia walked around the compound by herself. She was not afraid of being outside alone in the large compound. She was aware that the security guards used circuited monitors to keep an eye on activities within the five-acre compound, and she always carried her cell phone, just in case she needed urgent help.

During her evening walks, she took time to reflect on her life. She was thankful for what she had achieved since completing her university education.

Now, in her third year of work with the Mwasimba Group of Companies, she had lifted her family out of poverty. Joy had completed her degree program from the national university. Silas was pursuing his engineering degree study program, and her other three younger brothers were in school, rarely sent home for lack of school fees.

Mariko, her father, had left his tedious job of buying and selling livestock for meagre profits. He was now the proprietor of Mariko & Family Stores in his village.

Further, she was now married after a long struggle which involved going against the wish of her father. Mariko had wanted her to relocate back to the village to get married to a local schoolteacher. Sophia did not want that, though her staying in the city was no better. Richie had pursued her every day, at a time when she did not wish to be involved in romance or marriage, aspects she believed would distract her from her job and career advancement.

She was now married Richie, a manager, a millionaire and eventually heir to part of the vast Mwasimba Group of Companies.

Sophia aroused herself from dozing off while seated on a bench in the orchard. She pondered what her life would be like if she resigned from work. Would she be comfortable to use the credit and debit cards Richie had given her and not worry about repayment of the bills?

She heaved herself up from the bench and strolled on. She reminded herself that unlike before, her father could now use profits from his shop to pay school fees for his children, the three younger sons. Joy would pay university fees for Silas.

She involuntarily tilted her head upwards, like she was in prayer. All her facial muscles relaxed, in response to the realization that if she implemented her new plan, she would be free from worries about money. She would then focus on her new family, her husband, and the baby due in less than three months.

She walked back into the house, smiled at the kitchen staff before she left for the dining room where she joined Patience who was taking tea.

~~~~~~

Richie found it hard to explain how October went by so fast, though he was happy with the launch of AMME during the last week of the month.

The launch lasted three days and drew participants from twenty-one of the fifty-four-plus countries of Africa. Most of the participants were senior executives from business firms seeking to understand what influence their businesses had on global financial markets, and how global events in turn affected their businesses.

The first day of the launch featured presentations from invited guests. On day two Richie made two presentations, one on the influence of the global stock exchange on businesses the world over. The second presentation focused on the specific services that AMME would offer firms in Africa.

The morning of day three was for one-on-one consultations with Richie and other staff of the Mwasimba Company. There was also membership registration by
~~~~~~

interested businesses. The launch concluded with a sumptuous dinner and drinks to which staff from the Mwasimba Group of Companies were invited.

Richie had no idea how tired he was, until he arrived home on Thursday evening, at the end of the launch of AMME.

When he voiced his tiredness, letting Sophia know he would sleep in on Friday, he was surprised by her response: "Hope you will not mind if you find me home with you."

His lips parted, but no words came out. He had wanted to ask for a repeat of her words. He abandoned the idea, afraid that a question could make her change her mind about staying home with him on Friday.

He embraced her until she complained. "Your tight grip will stop blood flow to my heart."

He released her. "Sorry. I have missed you so much. I am afraid that my office work made me rare around you for many days."

Sophia pulled his hand to her lips. "I too missed you. Tomorrow, I will serve you breakfast in bed. You need to rest." She kissed his fingers, one after the other.

She was quiet, wishing she could inform Richie of the decision she had reached - to ask her father to pay school fees for his children. She did not, first she needed to consult with her father, establish if he had enough savings to pay the school fees.

~~~~~~

On Friday morning Sophia was surprised that without an alarm clock, she did not wake up until nine o'clock when hunger could not let her sleep anymore.

Not wanting to spend energy getting ready for the day, she did what she knew was possible, but she had so far resisted indulging in. She called Theresa, and five minutes later, there was a knock on the bedroom door.

Theresa left a trolley full of assorted breakfast items by the bedroom door. Sophia wheeled it into the room.

As they ate breakfast, Richie noticed Sophia was energetic and happier compared to other days. At first, he attributed her happiness to the extra two hours of sleep she had enjoyed, an idea he disqualified on recalling she had not appeared this energetic and happy on weekends, when she habitually slept for more hours.

He wondered if her happiness was what he had read in one of the books on pregnancy and parenthood. That expectant mothers suddenly became cheerful in the third and final trimester of their pregnancy, a natural occurrence, for the woman would soon have a baby, a gift.

"You look so lost. Already missing your new department?" Sophia's words startled Richie back into reality.

He leaned forward and kissed her. "I was having a nice dream, how life would be if we never had a reason to leave the house, simply stay in bed."
~~~~~~

"One day we can do that, after working hard and saving enough money," she said.

"I doubt if there's a time called 'enough money'. Enough is what you and I decide or define."

There was a moment of silence as Richie refilled their cups with tea. Sophia appeared reflective. She was mulling over the words from Richie on the meaning of having enough money. "You could be right."

She waited for him to ask a question. When he did not, she sipped more tea, put the cup down then laughed. "I meant your definition of having enough money. Sometimes, I think we could be having more money than we need."

Richie picked a large chunk of his spinach and cheddar cheese omelette and stuffed his mouth.

Sophia looked at him, amused. "I see you are very hungry."

A nod of head gave Sophia reason to laugh again. Richie added more food into his mouth. This was his way of having time to reflect on Sophia's words as he wondered if by having more money than we need, she meant the Mwasimba family or just the two of them.

He swallowed, sipped tea, and put the cup back on the saucer. "I could be with you on that. Sometimes we work too hard for money. We already have what we need, no need for you to stay in employment."

Sophia placed her left hand on his arm. "To help you reduce the amount of money we have, I will take a longer maternity leave."

Richie lifted Sophia's chin as he lowered his head and kissed her. "Thank you, my love. I fully understand. You must be tired."

She held his hand and pushed it away from her chin. "I am not tired. I am pregnant with our growing baby."

"Sure," Richie said before he took another large bite of omelette, as he waited to hear details of her maternity leave. He lifted cup of tea closer to his mouth to shield his smiley face. "Did Michael say who will help with work while you are on leave?" he asked, to get Sophia to talk, and reveal if she had already begun her leave.

She went and drew back the window curtains to let in more of the morning sunshine. "You just read my mind. I was thinking of how to make a smooth transition, one that would allow me to get back to work after my maternity leave."

He exhaled, loudly and noted the questioning expression on Sophia's face. Her eyebrows pulled in, almost touching the bridge of her nose. She asked, "What is worrying you? Is it because both of us thought of the same issue, work?"

"Not really." He rested his hand on her shoulder. "Let's go to the sofa, that way you will not complain of back pain from sitting on that hard chair," as he pointed to her chair. They went and sat at the two-seater sofa. "I would like to hear your thoughts on how you will handle the transition," he said.

"I have too many ideas in my head. I asked Liz if she can upgrade to my duties while I am away. We will find a student intern to manage the front desk.

Richie held Sophia's left hand and intertwined his fingers with hers. He held her wedding ring and tried to turn it around, without success. He tried to pull it out but stopped when she winced. "That was painful."

He stared at her. "That must hurt. I will help you slip it out before your finger turns numb."

Sophia placed her left hand on his thigh. "Remove it?"

"Yes. Would you like us to try?"

She whispered a yes.

Richie stood up and helped her to her feet, they went to the bathroom. At the sink, he plugged in the stopper, opened the tap, and added liquid soap. "Let me know when it hurts, and I will stop," he said as he immersed her fingers in the soapy water, massaged the finger, and slid the ring out.

She held her hand in front of her eyes and blew air onto her relieved ring finger. "I wonder what people will say."

"Sometimes, just put your comfort first, before other people. What does the pastor always say at church about loving yourself first, after which it will be easy to love others?"

When she laughed, he added. "Do not try to love everyone, only me and our babies."

Sophia laughed as she inspected her ring-less finger, again. "Thanks. I will take a quick shower and go outside before the morning sun turns too hot."

Richie nodded a yes, though he could not believe that their chat on her extended leave was already over. He had hoped they would go back to the sofa, for her to tell him when she planned to start her leave.

Chapter 26

They stopped at the dining room, greeted Patience before Sophia sat down and said, "Sorry, we left you to eat by yourself."

Patience placed the cup she was holding on the table. "I assumed you had eaten when I found only my cup here."

Richie pulled a chair beside Sophia. "Today my wife served me breakfast in the bedroom, that's the reason she is too late to go to work."

From the side of her eye, Sophia noticed that Patience had looked at her left hand twice.

Sophia placed her left hand flat on the table and spread out the fingers. "Serving you breakfast was of tremendous benefit to my finger." She waved the hand in front of Patience, her act sending Richie into loud laughter.

"I have been wondering if it never hurt. I knew you would remove it soon or go to a jewelry store to have it cut," Patience said.

"What? To be cut?" Sophia asked.

"Yes, to save your finger. Next time remember to remove the ring earlier or have it adjusted, usually by the third month."

Sophia turned to Richie and winked. She was amused that Patience was already thinking of more children, even before the first one was born.

Richie held his left hand remarkably close to Sophia's face. "I am now the only one married. Are you feeling jealousy?"

She shoved his hand away with her forehead. Getting up she said, "Our destination was outside, to enjoy the morning sun."

Patience watched them as they walked out through the side door of the living room, to the veranda at the back of the house.

After five minutes of strolling, they sat in a gazebo at the far side of the orchard garden. Once they were comfortable on the brown reed chairs, Richie looked up into the roof. "When do you plan to start training Liz?"

Sophia lifted both hands upwards and yawned. "I informed Michael. I have also asked Liz if PA duties interest her. She will confirm on Monday. If she agrees, I will start training her for the next one month."

"That will take you into December?" Richie asked in a raised voice.

"Yes, December, when I start my leave"

Richie wanted to argue, tell Sophia that she was too tired to work until December, but he chose not to. He recalled that since last night she had shared only information that brought happiness to his heart. From choosing not to go to work that day, to her decision to extend her maternity leave. She might have more good news for him the rest of the day.

He placed her hand onto his lap. "I support your plan to train Liz well, for you might need her sooner, or more in the future."

She chuckled. "Today, you and Mum are on a similar wavelength."

He squeezed her hand. "What?"

"She's already thinking of another pregnancy to remove the ring, and you are thinking of Liz being of help in future maternity leaves. Does that mean we can start discussions on the next baby, before this one is born?"

He stood up and assisted Sophia to get to her feet. "Nothing excites me like hearing the word more babies. As you rightly put it, Mum and I are on the same page when it comes to babies, children. Let us make more, I promise to love each one fully."

He hugged her closer to his chest, as close as her bulging belly could allow. "We need to fill all the empty rooms in the house, give Mum more hours in her kitchen, cooking for you and her grandkids."

She tickled his neck. "I fully support your idea. Mum taking care of our children means I will have enough time to work harder in the office."

Richie's lips parted, but no words came out. He held her by the small of her back as they reached the front side of the house.

Not wanting to linger over Sophia's words about going back to work, he distracted his thoughts. "May we ask Mum to take us to go shop for baby items?"

She inhaled and exhaled, audibly. "Who buys baby items before the baby is born?"

"Trust me. Sorry, not me. Have faith in God, and then Dr. Rajur," Richie said as he moved two steps away and stood in front of Sophia. "Please take a good look at me."

She stared at his face, before she lowered her neck and inspected him down to his feet, clad in open brown leather shoes as she heard him add, "Dr. Rajur's baby." He chuckled. "And remember to inspect Nick the next time you see him. He is the other baby, delivered by the doctor."

Sophia beamed as she lifted her pointer finger to his lips, to stop him from uttering more words.

He took one step forward and stood beside her. "You agree that we can go admire baby items, only green and yellow." He smiled, "Unless you want a scan to reveal if it is blue or pink baby items."

She held Richie's hand as they walked into the house. "One thing I am sure of, the baby will be one of the two, no third choice." She squeezed his hand. "We may go window shopping. Just promise we will be back for my afternoon nap, which I must have since I am home."

Richie stretched out his pinkie finger. "Is that how ladies seal a deal?" He entangled his pinkie with that of

Sophia. "I promise. Our destination will be to just one shop, Watoto R Us."

Sophia placed a hand on her chest while she stared at Richie. She had wanted to ask why they should go to the most expensive baby store in the city and the whole country.

She suppressed her urge. She had remembered her resolution that her father needed to take back his family's financial responsibility - paying school fees for his children. That way, she could spend her money on her family, with little worry.

She had heard stories that Watoto R Us had a room reserved for expectant mothers to sit and recover lost energy from too much shopping.

The shop also had a nursery section where nursing mothers could choose a comfortable chair and breastfeed their babies. She would go see for herself, a chance to enter the store that she only knew from the outside.

Chapter 27

Richie revised his schedule for November after Sophia insisted, she would stay at work to train Liz. His initial plan had been to take her on a surprise visit, to an exclusive club to celebrate her birthday.

The local trip came up after Dr. Rajur advised him against flying her to Europe, Richie's earlier plan. The doctor recommended they could go on a road trip but avoid bumpy roads.

"Any plans for your future weekends?" Richie asked as they had breakfast one Sunday morning. His parents had left for church while he stayed home with Sophia in line with Patience's advice not to trouble herself waking up early to go to church.

Holding a glass of fresh juice near her mouth, Sophia spoke without turning her head. "Any plans other than waiting for the baby?" She asked as she put the glass on the table. She smoothed her stomach. "And whispering to the baby to stop kicking me so hard?"

Richie placed his hand on the right side of her stomach. "Show me where the baby has kicked you. I need to provide a fatherly warning."

They both laughed.

He smoothed her stomach. "Would you like to go on another Safari?"

"Reserve that invitation for next year this time, when the baby will be old enough to go on a Safari with us."

Richie agreed with her, mainly because he had received the information he needed, that she had no big plans for the coming weekends until the baby was born. He would now go ahead with his surprise birthday party for her, in two weeks' time. Whereas her actual birthday date fell on a Thursday, he would instead celebrate it two days later, on a Saturday.

He was glad when she left for the bedroom to have a siesta following lunch. He made a phone call to Rose, the event organizer that the family used for smaller parties other than weddings. After answering most of her questions about preferred colours, venue and number of guests, Richie informed Rose that Patience would be her point of contact for any other questions.

On Thursday, the day of Sophia's birthday, Richie gave her a card and a bouquet of flowers to mark the day. Patience had the dining table decorated with side candles for dinner, and Nick joined them in wishing her a happy birthday.

Sophia was not privy to the arrangements that were made during the week while she was away at work. Patience had called and invited her sons and daughters-in-law and Richie's cousins and some of his close friends. She had also invited Joy and Silas.

Patience asked Joy to invite Justine and some of their cousins. They had an agreement that it was a surprise, so none of them was to mention the party to Sophia.

On Friday night, Richie informed Sophia that he was tired and would not mind sleeping in on Saturday morning. He asked Theresa to deliver breakfast to their bedroom.

When Sophia tried to object, he reminded her that they had eaten breakfast in the bedroom for she needed to reserve her energy for an afternoon visit to the club where she could walk the vast grounds.

Richie's goal was to make sure that Sophia did not hear or see any of the activities taking place inside and outside the house that morning. There were people setting up tents, seats, and food. Richie played soft music in the bedroom to block out any suspicion-raising sounds in the compound.

At midday, she showered and dressed in a free-flowing magenta Oscar de la Renta dress. The bodice was embroidered with splayed white flower petals, each seeming to emerge out of the fabric, so well fitted, one had to wonder where the stitching was hidden. A grey sheer scarf not only complimented her sleeveless dress but would for sure keep off the afternoon wind and any roving mosquitoes.

She held her hair to the top of her head, enhancing her height. Her Freesia-coloured three-inch-block-heeled Acne ankle boots and matching Bea Valdes clutch and cowries-shell earrings brought her whole being into one centerpiece. She was ready to leave for the club, perhaps for the last time before the baby's anticipated arrival in January.

Richie put on a tailcoat suit and matching hat, to Sophia's surprise. Even though he was already well-known for his designer suits, leather shoes and fancy cars, he looked remarkable that Saturday afternoon.

He switched off the music in the bedroom, allowing Sophia to hear the music and people chatting outside.

She stared at him, eyes wide open.

He held her hand to relieve her of the purse she had picked to match her dress. "You might not need this, but we can carry it to complete your attire and stunning look."

He kissed her, "Happy birthday my dear wife, my best friend. Please promise to ask me only one question on this joyful day."

With one side of her mouth pushed upwards, into a forced grin, she held his hand. "I am very confused with your words and the strange noise from outside."

"We agreed on one question only, please ask me before we go outside." Richie looked at her, crooked his left arm at the elbow which she held onto.

She leaned closer. "Please tell me what is going on."

He lowered his head closer to her ear. "I must tell you, because the doctor said we avoid anything that can raise your blood pressure."

He wiggled the fingers of his right hand. "There is a small birthday gathering outside, at the garden, for you. Come let's go celebrate." He said as he guided her hesitant feet towards the bedroom door. They walked out.

As they reached the family room, Richie covered Sophia's eyes with his right hand.

She voiced her concern. "If you cover my eyes, it means I will spend a lot of energy, struggling to place each foot on the floor."

He removed his hand. "Agreed, no need to make you stumble, or compel you to ask me more questions. Yet, you've used up all your chances." He winked at her.

Sophia paused and marveled at the setup in the two dining rooms and the sitting room. As they approached the outside through the main door, the crowd at the tent went silent and everyone focused on the couple.

Sophia looked at the people seated under the tent and stood still.

Her feet did not move, and Richie had no idea what to do other than lift her and walk to the tent. But he knew better, such an action would be risky, in case she fell. He maintained a grin on his face, which turned into a smile when he saw Beauta walk their direction.

Beauta, dressed in a mandarin orange Ferragamo slip dress and the plum shade of the Rihanna Style DSquared heels, reached and greeted them before she complimented Richie "It's not too late for you to change careers, you were made to model clothes."

He flashed her thumbs-up, "I can start tomorrow if you open a clothing line."

Beauta spread out both arms for Sophia. "You look lovely. That dress fits like it was designed and tailor-made just for you. We need a photo for one of those magazines."

She embraced Sophia. "We must chase Richie away. I want to walk with you to the tent."

Beauta's loud whisper was meant for Richie. He obeyed by walking to the tent where he arrived and tipped his hat and waved at the crowd of about thirty guests. He kissed Georgina, Bill's wife, before sitting on one of the two adjacent empty chairs.

Richie watched and wondered what magic words Beauta had used to get Sophia to walk to the tent, holding hands. The two paused on reaching the tent as a cameraman took a succession of photos.

Sophia glanced at the visitors, waved at Patty, and then Justine as Joy ululated, to the amusement of the guests.

Sophia embraced Beauta before she went and sat on the vacant chair between Georgina and Richie. As soon as she made herself comfortable, she saw Mwasimba emerge from the house and walk towards the tent.

She turned sideways to Richie, and her lips parted like she wanted to say something. Richie held her head between his hands and kissed her on the mouth. The crowd cheered. When he released her, he went and greeted his father who then motioned Richie back to his seat.

Mwasimba greeted all present and welcomed them to his home and the party.

Patience handed him a glass of wine which he lifted to a toast. He informed the guests that he would not stay but would be back later for dinner. He lifted the glass of wine one more time in the direction of Richie and Sophia, took two sips, before leaving for the car waiting in the driveway.

Sophia relaxed as time passed. She walked around the party grounds chatting with the guests.

At around five o'clock, Rose, the party organizer left her seat and walked into the house. She re-emerged, followed by two kitchen staff carrying a cake with a large number 26 at the center.

Before cutting the cake, Sophia looked at the crowd, then at the cameraman. "If you take a photo of this…" as she pointed to the number on the cake, "All the people will know how old I am. Please do not." The crowd broke into the popular happy birthday song.

After they quieted, Rose served Sophia the first piece of cake before she sliced the rest for the guests.

When Bill received a piece of the cake, he called out loudly, "Sophia, the person you should worry about knowing your age is the baby."

She responded by involuntarily touching her stomach, like she had been reminded she was pregnant. She tilted her head back as she heard Bill complete the sentence. "He/she will always look at the photo to know how old you were."

Bill stopped talking when Richie stood up and looked to his direction. "Too much whisky already, or should I bring you more?"

Bill growled at Richie, "Whisky is for the evening. Don't forget that Chairman invited us to the men's gathering."

At sunset, the guests had separated into undefined groups. Richie and Sophia walked around chit-chatting the various groups.

When they reached Georgina, she unhooked Sophia's hand from Richie's arm. "It is boring to have your wife with you all the time, leave the birthday girl to us."

Richie kissed Georgina on the cheek before he walked away without uttering a word. He went to the back of the house where he joined Enock, Bill, Sam, Michael and four other men.

Michael stared at Richie. "I have a feeling that if you set your wife free, she will do exactly what you have been pleading for her to do."

The rest of the people laughed as Michael added, "Tonight, I will ask Chairman to send you back to me for more mentoring."

Richie held two fingers up, a sign of peace.

As the group broke into more laughter, Richie scanned the space. "If you continue with that laughter, more people will join us, and then we will start to fight for oxygen." He pulled a chair and made himself comfortable.

Richie acknowledged the men with a nod of head. "Hope none of you took Mike's words seriously, especially those of you unable to convince your girlfriends to marry you." He turned to Michael and winked. "Nothing makes a man proud like walking in public with his wife holding onto him."

Michael took a sip from his glass before his lips parted, like he wanted to speak, but Richie spoke ahead of him. "Ask Mike or watch him when he walks around with our beautiful Beauta. He has so far avoided that to save you guys from drooling."

The men shouted back a mixture of yes and no, giving Richie reason to say more. "My brother is a very considerate man, to all the single men here." He waved his hand towards Enock.

Michael stared at Richie until laughter from the group subsided before he said, "Thanks. I thought you had not noticed." Next, he addressed the group. "Boys, Richie has just revealed the secret. If you watch me with my Beauta, there is no way you will not soon call us to your wedding. That is how I got these two to marry," he pointed from Bill to Richie. "Otherwise, they would still be eligible bachelors, like the rest of you."

All heads turned as three Range Rovers drove into the compound. Mwasimba and some of his age-mates alighted from the chauffeured vehicles.

Richie walked over and shook hands with each of the five men before he led them into the living room.

Patience welcomed Mwasimba and his visitors into the dining room for dinner.

~~~~~~

Sophia was surprised that it was already two in the morning, thirteen hours since she had walked out of their bedroom. Except for the frequent need to sit down or use the toilet, she had remained awake and alert.
~~~~~~

Richie and Sophia had retreated to their bedroom after seeing off most of the guests and offering accommodation to those who were too inebriated.

Patience had made an announcement earlier, encouraging the guests to enjoy the party, including alcohol, and, she had enough rooms for anyone who would need a place to sleep. To the few who had laughed off her offer, she had given motherly advice. "Please respect the great people manning the gate. Come ask me if they refuse to open for you to leave."

While in the bedroom, Sophia was surprised that Richie was not tired. He offered to help her bathe and change into warm evening clothes.

"You're too sober compared to your friends. What happened?" She asked.

He supported her back with one arm while smoothing her stomach with the other. "Please tell me if you taste any beer," he kissed her.

She sniffed the air. "I am not the police breathalyzer, though—" She kissed him. "You are right on that one. I now understand why we almost ran out of juice."

He cuddled her, shifting his neck for a soft bite of her earlobe. "Maybe your sense of taste was corrupted by the cake you ate. Do you not smell any alcohol?"

She shook her head to indicate no, as Richie explained: "I am not a fan of alcoholic drinks, as you already know. Better still, no way would I drink while assisting the birthday girl to welcome her guests."

Sophia released herself from his cuddling "Mr. Richie Mwasimba, I do not know how to thank you. How did you pull such a grand surprise party together?"

She chewed on his bottom lip. "I enjoyed every minute of the day after recovering from the shock of seeing so many people in the beautifully decorated grounds." Her top and bottom eyelashes met to conceal the tears wetting her eyes, tears of joy.

"Mum provided part of the service," Richie said as they left the bedroom and strolled back to the party. "I see you are not very tired. Come, be by my side as I toast to your birthday."

"If I sit down in the sofa, you will have to carry me to bed, which I discourage, since you have a bottle of wine in your hand." Sophia said as she held the armrest of the sofa and lowered herself onto the chair.

Richie watched her and only sat down after she had made herself comfortable.

From the corner of her eye, Sophia watched Bill, Michael, Sam, Enock and five other men seated around a coffee table with a crate of beer nearby.

After a short while, she excused herself and went to the bedroom. As she was getting into bed the door opened, and Richie walked in. "I'm here to sing you a lullaby."

Their eyes locked as the dimples on her face sank deeper, "So sweet of my husband. Please go back and enjoy the rest of the night with your many brothers," she said while pulling a bed sheet over her head.

Richie bent to reach her on the bed and kissed her good night. "Send me a message if our noise keeps you awake."

Chapter 28

The end of year mood had set in for many people. A time when students sit for end of school year exams, and parents make travel plans upcountry, to their rural homes in December.

Realizing that he was too focused on office work, Richie decided to help Sophia create fun for her December holidays and the birth of their baby in January. What are your plans now that the weekend is one day away?"

Not sure where the question was leading, Sophia said, "We can visit Joy and Silas, or my friend Justine."

"Tell Joy I will be there to taste her cooking." He chuckled, "Though I am certain that none of your siblings comes even close to you in terms of your excellent cooking."

Sophia held his left hand. "I had no idea you know my cooking. Mum prepares most of the meals, and when she's not around, Wekesa, the chef takes over."

"Have you forgotten the number of times you fed me? When I used to follow you to your house, trying extremely hard to win your heart?" He asked as he wiped a finger across his forehead, to clear away imaginary sweat.

She tickled him on the armpit. "Interesting times those were. By the time we move to our house next year, my cooking skills would have become rusty."

He pulled her closer to his side. "That killer smile arrests all my senses." He sighed and released her, and they continued with their evening walk.

Richie became thoughtful. He had almost forgotten, or he had taken the idea of not moving to their residence for granted, as Sophia had not mentioned it for the last five months. He recalled from their last discussion, her request that they stay in the north wing until the baby was born, which was now less than two months away.

He was relieved on remembering what his mother once told him about babies – they keep new mothers so busy that they forget to pursue other planned activities. He comforted himself that once the baby arrived, Sophia would get busy learning how to care for a newborn.

She would not have time to consider adding the task of moving homes and managing new house workers to her already full hands. They would have at least six more months in the north wing. Sophia would need adequate time to get used to her new life of motherhood.

Richie panicked as he recalled what she had said about taking leave from her PA tasks – that, she would go back to work after six months. Scratching his head, he wondered how life was going to be with a new baby, moving to a new residence, having new employees in the house, Sophia going back to work and him managing AMME, the new department, with remarkably high chances of becoming its director.

He involuntarily shook his head, prompting Sophia to squeeze his arm. "Is everything okay?"

"I guess so. I have been dreaming about our new life in the next few months. Does your mind ever take you that far?"

She lowered herself onto a bench under a guava tree. "Over-thinking is not good for the baby. The only thoughts I have are of happiness—"

Richie joined her on the bench, and she continued to speak. "In the beginning, I had this fear that Liz would not want to disrupt her easy life by stepping into my PA shoes." She chuckled. "Surprises do happen. She is overly concerned about me and the baby. She is ready to help."

Richie knew that voicing what was in his mind would not help the situation. He had wanted to ask Sophia to start her maternity leave immediately. He hesitated, decided he would wait until Sophia completed her maternity leave, and then ask her to extend her leave. "Good to hear that Liz is growing up. She sometimes gets me concerned about her lack of interest in furthering her career." He said.

Sophia tried to stand up but sat back. Richie stood up and extended both hands to her. "Will you go to work tomorrow or stay home and rest?"

She parted her braids to one side of the head. "Sorry, I forgot to tell my husband, that I now work four days a week. I plan to reduce them to three, two, one and then I will be on full leave from December."

"Thanks for making the decision. A good sign of things to come," Richie said, though his wish was different. If Sophia had consulted him, he would have asked her to work one or two days a week or just take leave and stay home.

They walked behind the north wing part of the house in silence. As they approached from the side of the kitchen, Richie said, "I remember doctor Rajur mention that firstborn babies can arrive earlier than their expected date. Do you still want to risk working to the last day?"

Sophia paused her step and made eye contact with Richie. "Your question reminds me of a song we used to sing while learning English at school."

He moved closer to her. "I have not heard you sing, except at church. Please sing the song for me."

"It was a silly song. We called out someone's name and asked them where they were born."

"Mmhhh."

"The person was given options to choose from—kitchen, toilet, bathroom, church." Sophia laughed before she added. "Those were...," she lifted he left hand in front of her eyes and folded her pinkie, then her ring finger, her engagement finger, and her pointer finger as she said, "Four choices." She waved a thumbs-up. "You and I will bring the thumb into the count, if I work until the baby is born in the office."

Richie held her hand, and they slowly took the remaining paces to reach the door into the house. "I could have laughed if the idea of our baby being born in the office was not closer to happening."

~~~~~~~

On Saturday morning Sophia joined Patience at the table for breakfast. They took their time eating and talking about general topics, including the setting up of the baby's room.

"How will that work, parents in a different room, away from a newborn?" Sophia asked when Patience suggested setting up the baby's nursery in a different room from their bedroom.

Patience lifted her cup and sipped tea before she said, "I hear that is what mothers do nowadays, have their baby in a nearby room and use a baby monitor to know whether the baby is asleep or awake."

Sophia decided not to engage further on the topic. There was no need to argue on where her baby would sleep, she would bring the baby into their bedroom. That was what mothers did—her mother, and most probably Patience. "We will not be here for lunch. We're going to visit Joy and Silas."

"Pass my greetings them. Tell Joy to visit more often now that she drives. No more excuses over how to get here, and not wanting to be picked up and dropped off."

"I will pass your message to her." Sophia said as she watched a grey Porsche Boxster come to a stop on the driveway near the orchard.
~~~~~~~

A moment later, there was a knock on the front door, Patience called Theresa to open the door for a visitor. She let Enock in.

Sophia got concerned knowing that Enock's arrival meant they would delay leaving the house, and hence arrive at Joy's place later than their agreed time.

Enock looked at Sophia, then Patience. "Did I interrupt mother and daughter talk?"

"Oh no," Patience said, getting up from her chair. "Have you ever heard of a son interrupting his family?" She asked before she invited him to join them at the table.

Enock walked to the opposite side of the table and kissed Sophia on the cheek. "How are you and our baby?"

"As fine as ever," she said as she watched him walk towards Richie who had entered the family room.

"I told you I would arrive ahead of you, and I did." Enock called to Richie as he fisted his hand and met with a similar one from Richie, in greeting.

Richie looked in the direction of the dining table. "My wife left me in bed, the reason I refused to wake up until you insisted."

"Go back to bed. Enock will take me to Joy's place," Sophia called out from the dining room.

Richie and Enock reached the dining room and pulled out chairs as Richie said to Sophia. "No way will I allow him to walk around with you." He winked at Enock. "He might receive compliments and blessings reserved only for me," Richie said as he tapped on his chest, in praise.

They all laughed, before Patience stood up. "Have a lovely day. I need to get ready, as I am going with your father for a luncheon."

"Have a nice day Mum, see you later," Sophia said as Patience walked off, past the living room and into the west side of the house.

Chapter 29

Joy answered the door with the first knock and swung it open. "Everyone, please get out of the way." She looked at Sophia and giggled. "We might even have to call the mason to tear down the door for my sister to walk through."

She checked Sophia from head to toe. "You know what I like best, your baby-like skin, a nice glow, and your designer clothes. Keep it up."

Sophia extended her hands to either side of Joy's ears and pulled upwards in a mock pinch.

Richie interjected. "Your sister is dressed and fed by her new mother. I see you like everything about her. Good."

As Sophia walked inside, Joy, with arms held akimbo, tilted her head up and made eye contact with Richie.

Richie did not budge, he locked eyes with Joy. "I will soon find you a good mother-in-law, though nothing close to my wife's," he said as he accepted Joy's hand in a greeting.

He turned to his left and said, "Joy, meet Enock my buddy. Enock, meet Joy, Sophia's younger sister."

Enock extended a hand in greeting, "We have met before." She accepted his hand.

Richie looked over his shoulder. "All you have to remember is that you met through me, I introduced both of you." He winked at Enock.

The two men stepped into the living room. Richie scanned the walls. "Where is the Silas, still attached to his engineering projects?" He asked before sitting down next to Sophia on the three-seater sofa.

Sophia pressed on Richie's knee for support as she stood up and walked to one side of the living room. "Joy never stops to amaze. I was here a few weeks back, and now I see yet another piece of artwork," she said as Silas walked in and gave her a one-shoulder hug. "Hi sister, you look your best each time I see you."

"Thanks, Silas. For now, focus on your books." She touched her stomach. "You have a long way to go before society allows you to start thinking about how nice women in my state look."

Everyone in the room broke into laughter.

Silas gave Sophia a soft pat on the shoulder. "I am in total agreement, especially with my daily school assignments. I should have chosen a more relaxed study program." He said before he greeted Richie, then Enock. "I am Silas, Sophia's brother and Joy's boss."

Richie stood up and admonished him, "Saying Joy's boss many times will ruin your sister's market, which right now is nearing max." He went to the kitchen where Joy had retreated to check on the food she was preparing.

~~~~~~

After lunch, Richie, Enock and Silas left to spin Richie's Jaguar.

Sophia followed Joy into her bedroom to admire her latest collection of designer items. She sat on the edge of Joy's bed.

While busy pulling out clothes and hanging them back into the wardrobe, Joy asked casually, "Have you heard from Mama lately?"

"What about her? Yes, I talked with her." Sophia tilted her head upwards as if she was trying to recall the last time she talked with Stella. "That was on Tuesday. Is Grandma still asking about me? Please tell her there's no way I can travel home now." Sophia chuckled while involuntarily massaging her growing belly, now shy of eight months.

Holding onto her Coach Leather tote bag, Joy said, "If the mountain cannot go to Mimi, Mimi must come to the mountain."

Sophia laughed. "Your time of being called a mountain will come. When will you introduce your boyfriend to me for vetting?"

"Which boyfriend? The ones I can handle are busy putting in fifteen hours in the office to get their dream promotion."

Joy walked back to the wardrobe. "I like the silent competition at my place of work. People are very friendly,
~~~~~~

yet everyone is working hard to outsmart the other." She said as she went and sat at her dresser chair.

"I guess that's how the successful companies in town keep flourishing. Ask me. I can whisper to you how hard the Mwasimba sons work. They leave the house early and go back home only when they are too tired to add something new."

"Richie must be happy that you are home with his mother while he's away toiling," Joy said as she went to her wardrobe. "There's a dress here you should see. I got it from a workmate who traveled to the UK last week."

Sophia looked at Joy and wondered how to tell her that she was still working. "What would you do if you married into a family with no struggles for money?"

Joy laughed as she walked back, holding a bareback red dress by Michael Costello. "You will be right if you tried to guess for me. I will travel to London to buy clothes with my money." She waved the red dress in front of Sophia. "I will use an Amex card, to be precise."

"That means you would stop working?"

Joy handed the dress to Sophia. "Not until he succeeds, makes my belly like yours. Then I will use the chance to stay home, like you."

Sophia admired the dress. She inspected it, turned it around, smoothed the material and squished the fabric between her fingers for a better feel. "You are mistaken—"

"What? Isn't the dress groovy enough?"

"I still go to work. I am currently training the person who will hold my tasks for the time I will be away, on leave."

Joy made eye contact with Sophia. "Are you sure you are not breaking the Mwasimba rules, by going to work. Does Richie support your crazy idea?"

Sophia made an uncomfortable move on the bed, like the soft mattress had suddenly become hard and rough to sit on. "There are no rules at Mwasimba's about going to work."

Joy extended a hand to receive the dress that Sophia was handing back to her. Joy said, "I know one thing for sure, that the rich prefer their women to stay home, more so when pregnant." She pulled out a clothes hanger and draped the dress in it. "It is an unwritten rule. Do you want to be the first one to break it?"

Sophia chuckled as she struggled to stand up from the bed.

Joy sat still and looked at her until she got to her feet and walked towards the bathroom.

Joy stared as Sophia lifted one foot after the other until she entered the en-suite bathroom and the door closed behind her.

As her pregnancy progressed, Sophia visited the toilet several times each day.

While using the toilet, she pondered Joy's words about breaking the rules of her new family. She worried if that was the message Richie had been trying to communicate to her since their honeymoon, with his persistent requests to resign from work. She did what she had no plan of doing, lowered herself fully on the toilet seat and stayed there, ruminating, until she heard a knock on the door. "Are you okay in there, or should I call your mister?"

"Coming," Sophia called back. She knew well that any hesitation on her side would get Joy to start struggling with the bathroom door, assuming that Sophia was incapacitated.

When Sophia opened the door and returned to the bedroom, she could hear people talking and laughing in the living room, a sign that the men were back from their car ride.

She left the bedroom and joined Joy in the kitchen where she was preparing tea. "Did Mama mention if Mimi is willing to travel to the city? It would be good to have her around," Sophia said.

Joy made a quick glance into the living room and back to the tea on the cooker. "It will only be better for her to come after you stop pushing your big stomach to the office."

She looked at Sophia and could tell that her sister was not pleased with her words, so she added, "Maybe we can ask one of your drivers to go bring Mimi here. I remember your pregnancy was foretold by her at your wedding."

"Whose wedding is coming up?" Richie asked, announcing his arrival in the kitchen.

Joy pointed Sophia to a chair before she answered Richie's question. "Surprise, surprise that wedding bells are still ringing in Richie's head, long after his wedding." She chuckled, "Time to change it to baby bells."

"Enock, I know you fear kitchen floors. Come over here, today only." Richie called out.

Enock appeared promptly as summoned and leaned against the kitchen door jamb.

Richie lifted Enock's left hand. "I see all your fingers are free, and Joy here…," he pointed towards Joy. "She has wedding bells ringing in her ears. I doubt if you want to let that opportunity pass by you."

Enock winked at Joy.

Joy looked at Sophia, then Richie. "Enock appears to be a nice guy, how would he manage a girl like me?"

Richie joined Enock in laughter before he paused and addressed him, "Enock, the boxing ring is open. Are you ready for the challenge?"

Joy lifted the saucepan lid to check the simmering tea while she said. "The kitchen has suddenly become small." She turned to Richie's direction. "Please lift your wife out first. She will tell you how Mimi wants to come and see the birth of my niece or nephew." She switched off the burner. "She will be thrilled that you acted on the command she gave at your wedding."

As they laughed and walked out of the kitchen, Richie looked over his shoulder to Joy in the kitchen. "Those wedding bells are ringing again. Enock, please, do something before Joy learns to love her office work too much."

"Her lunch was fantastic. Let's taste her tea next," Enock said as he followed Richie out of the kitchen.

Joy shouted from the kitchen, "Days of marrying cooks are long gone," as she sieved the tea into a flask.

Enock returned to the kitchen. "The day you come with me is the day you will miss the kitchen. I will unleash my cooking skills. Please accept me." he pleaded.

Joy went to the dining room where she placed a tray with a tea flask and cups.

Enock followed Joy to the dining room and stood at one end of the table. He observed keenly as she arranged cups from the tray onto coasters on the table.

Richie asked Sophia why she was so quiet. "Did you have your after-lunch siesta?" He asked, though he knew that would not have been possible while Sophia was with Joy. "Are you ready for your nap, or tea first?"

Sophia called out, "Joy, I no longer take tea, a cup of hot milk with Milo or something else without caffeine will do. Thanks in advance."

"Okay. I will prepare the drink for you before I call everybody else to the table."

"I will wait. Please serve the others first," Sophia said as she struggled to stand up from the sofa.

Enock noticed and took long strides to the living room. He arrived and extended a hand to her as Richie's hand reached Sophia's first. Enock protested. "Why not give me a chance to practice?"

Richie walked by Sophia's side to the dining room while he addressed Enock. "This part of life has no rehearsals, you only get the thrill while on stage, your own stage."

Enock followed them. "I will be there soon, with Joy. I know she will accept me."

Joy peeked out from the kitchen door, "Enock, no need to trouble trouble. What do they say about the trouble?"

Silas walked into the dining room. "Finally, my sister agrees that she is trouble."

Leaning onto the back of a dining seat with hands crossed, Enock stared at Silas. "One thing that gets real men out of bed each morning is the trouble out there in the world, pure pleasure."

Silas raised both hands in surrender. "I concur, fully."

Enock gawked at Joy as she walked into the dining room. He had developed a natural liking for her since their first encounter at Sophia's wedding, then at Sophia's birthday party. He would make more occasions to meet with her, for his wish was to win her heart.

Joy glared at Silas. "I am not trouble," as she placed a cup of hot Milo on the table, in front of Sophia."

Though Joy had liked Enock from the moment he appeared at her doorstep, she would not bring herself to show that to Richie and her siblings.

Sophia thanked Joy for the Milo before she turned to Silas. "Joy is the next best girl in town. You saw how fast she responded to my request for a hot beverage." Sophia smiled as she pointed Joy to a vacant seat next to Enock. "I will say grace before we enjoy our evening beverage."

After a prayer, Joy stood and served tea into the four empty cups. She started with that of Richie, followed by Silas, then Enock, before she served her cup.

They drank tea while chatting for the next one hour, discussing a variety of random topics.

Joy conveniently ignored questions about her place of work, preferring to talk mostly about the latest fashion in clothes and shoes.

Sophia was quiet on the drive back home, which Richie attributed to tiredness from clothes-showing and non-stop story-sharing by Joy. He would find a way to get Sophia into the right mood once they were inside the house, so he engaged Enock in a conversation.

Sophia was pensive, busy reflecting on the words from Joy about the rich not wanting their wives to stay in employment.

She wondered whether her going to work could have brought any embarrassment or shame to the Mwasimba family. But she comforted herself, certain that that could not be the case, since Patience had once told her that she raised her children to be free to make decisions on their choices in life. To her, that surely must include the choice she had made to stay in employment while pregnant.

Sophia also wondered if her choice to work was related to Richie's decision that they continue to reside in the north wing of his parents' house.

Chapter 30

Sophia was speechless. The bedroom adjacent to theirs had been converted into a charming nursery for a newborn baby.

A week earlier, the room had Superman poster-cuttings all over the walls, remnants of Richie's interests long before he was in high school.

Within the week, workers had come in, scrubbed old paint off the walls, and painted them a soft cream colour. They had converted the room into a baby's nursery, with all items, just as recommended in TV commercials.

While Sophia and Richie were busy at Akoth Towers, a truck branded Watoto R Us was driven into the Mwasimba's compound. Workers from the renowned baby store got busy wheeling into the house boxes and boxes of items.

When the bedroom was spotless clean, two women and a man from the design department of the children's store arrived in a minivan. They opened the boxes and arranged individual items in their optimal places within the room. The items were what Sophia had admired on her visits to the store.

Another look at the well-arranged items left Sophia stunned. She concluded that the baby shop must have cameras to capture all the items that shoppers put their hands on. How else did they get it so right on the exact items she had admired at the store?

Sophia walked around the room, her left hand on her bulging stomach.

When Richie noticed that she appeared tired, either from the standing or too much excitement, he kissed her and guided her out of the bedroom. "We can come back later, after you get a good rest.

They went and sat in the family room where Richie pulled a Scrabble game from a drawer for them to pass time.

She held Richie's hand. "You have not asked me why I went to work today, a Friday …, my off day."

"I am always happy with decisions and choices you make. Please tell me."

Sophia smiled, more out of surprise at the words uttered by Richie. One of the few things she could easily point out as Richie's weakness was his inability to consult her. He mostly made decisions on the assumption that they were the best for her, or for them. So, she was surprised when he said he was happy with decisions she made.

"I went to work today because it was my last day at the office." She intertwined her fingers with his. "Does that make you happy or sad? Your wife will be home before the indicated date of end of the month."

Richie stood up and extended a hand to Sophia. Once she was on her feet, he encircled his hands to her waist to give her steady support.

He kissed her until Patience interrupted. "I was coming to tell you that there is food on the table…in case you are ready to eat," She turned and walked out of the family room.

Sophia pressed her hand on Richie's chest to free from his hold. He cuddled her more, kissed her before he set her free and walked towards their bedroom.

Sophia joined Patience at the dining table. "Just so you know, it's my mistake that Richie is beyond words." She announced as she pulled a chair and sat. "It was an abrupt reaction after I told him that I am now on leave until June next year. I will go back to work in July."

Patience touched Sophia's hand, "Thank you for making that decision, it is the right decision."

Sophia served water into a glass and lifted it towards her mouth, then put it back on the table without taking a sip. "For you only, Richie's eyes were moist." She picked up the glass of water. "Just, so you know when he walks back."

Patience smiled in response.

Sophia reflected on the words from Patience, wondering if the right decision meant that Patience and the rest of the Mwasimba family had been waiting for her to resign or apply for early maternity leave.

"Thank you," Patience said as Richie emerged from the north wing.

Richie looked at his mother, then to Sophia. "Did you drink all the tea while I was away?"

Sophia tilted her neck backwards, in a bid to see Richie as he arrived at the table. "That will give me a chance to go prepare tea for you."

Richie stopped behind her, lowered his head, and kissed her before he supported the back of her head with both hands and guided it back to position. "I will be okay with that, you, standing in the kitchen for five minutes, just for me."

He pulled a chair next to her, picked an empty cup and held it close to her mouth. "Please serve me tea, now that you have no chance to go stand in the kitchen."

Patience smiled as Sophia stretched a hand towards the tea flask. Richie picked up the flask and handed it to her. She opened and served him tea while seated.

"Best wife on earth." Richie said as he lifted his cup to toast Sophia and then his mother.

Patience stared at Richie. "You sound like they made you a director today. Tell me, how's your new department coming along?"

He took a sip of tea as he watched his father walk into the dining room before he said, "Ask Chairman if they have made me a director without taking me through his vigorous probation period." He replaced the cup on the table. "Though another set of good news may not be good for my heart, it could stop my heartbeat," Richie said all the while looking in the direction of his father.

Mwasimba acknowledged everyone at the table with a greeting. He washed hands, pulled his usual dining chair, and sat, while in a monologue. "No one gets handed anything of value by me." He shifted his gaze to Richie. "You have six months to prove yourself, after that you may put in an application and wait for an interview."

"Yes sir," Richie said, his face engulfed in a smile.

Mwasimba glanced from Patience to Richie. "Something good happened that I need to know?"

"Richie is just happy that today is Friday, after a week of arduous work in the office." Sophia said, afraid that Richie, in his blissful mood could utter very personal words, creating discomfort at the table. She also worried that Richie might involuntarily share details of the many months he had spent trying to convince her to take an early maternity leave, and how she was finally on leave.

She considered pregnancy and maternity to be a private issue, not for discussion in the presence of her father-in-law.

Chapter 31

Sophia was reflective while on their Saturday evening walk. She wondered whether she had made the right decision to begin maternity leave earlier, within the first week of December, yet her estimated date of delivery was mid-January.

She also worried that Richie might not report to work on Monday. He had been elated, in a level of happiness only comparable to that which she had observed on their wedding day and during their honeymoon.

To ease him back to normality, Sophia said, "I will still be busy in those six months, taking care of the baby and packing, in readiness to move to our residence."

"I am not even thinking about relocations and whatever. After all we have the north wing and are yet to fill up its four bedrooms," Richie replied.

"Remember, we've taken over another bedroom in the house for the baby. I wish that nice arrangement was at our house."

With an even wider grin, he squeezed her hand. "That is not another bedroom. It's my childhood room. No need to bother yourself that we are taking over the Mwasimba's house." He kissed her earlobe. "Better if the room is occupied by our baby, rather than cobwebs," he said as they reached a wooden bench and sat down.

As Sophia's pregnancy progressed, their evening routine had changed. During the first and second trimesters, she could complete a thirty-minute walk without stopping to rest.

Now, with less than two months before her estimated delivery date, her steps were much slower, and she applied more energy, almost lumbering, with each step she took. What helped was the presence of benches considerately placed at random points in the grounds for anyone who wanted to sit under a tree, by the fruit orchard, or out in the sun.

She held onto the side of her stomach, as her eyebrows pulled in. "Oh, the intensity with which the baby kicks, makes me wonder why we did not just buy blue items."

"Please let me whisper to the baby, ask them not to harm my wife," Richie said as he bent his head towards her stomach.

She lifted his head away from her stomach while he continued to speak. "I need to remind the baby not to destroy the house for their future brothers and sisters." He cuddled her to his chest. "Is it that easy to guess that the baby will be a boy and not a girl?"

Sophia smiled before her eyebrows pulled together again, as she held the right side of her stomach. "I have my doubts that a baby girl could be this mean to their mother."

Both burst out into laughter. When the laughter subsided, she made eye contact with Richie. "Any plans on when you will take your paternity leave? In January, or in July when I resume work."

Richie stood up. "We will decide when the time comes." He extended a hand to help Sophia to her feet. "We need to get walking, otherwise your body slows down, and you start to ask me tough questions."

Sophia did not respond, she was thoughtful, concurring with how easily she tired. She smiled, grateful that she would not have reason to wake up early the next morning to go to work. No longer need to pull herself up from her office chair for frequent trips to use the toilet. She would now be able to stay in the bedroom all day if she wanted to, or sit in the family room, from where she would access the nearby toilet. "We should quicken our steps. I need to use the toilet."

They walked the remaining distance to the house in silence.

Over the last few weeks, Richie had learned that Sophia preferred silence until after she had emptied her bladder.

He reflected on her words about moving to their own residence. He squeezed her hand as he thought of how life would be, with him busy at work and Sophia at home with a newborn baby and new house helps. He worried over what she would do in case she or the baby felt unwell? Would she call him first, or Patience?

Richie contemplated various options on how best to convince her that they stay with his parents until the baby was old enough, perhaps two or three years.

What scared him most were thoughts on who would take care of the baby if Sophia insisted on returning to her job in July.

He pushed the kitchen door open, and Sophia hurried inside, leaving him behind.

He paused and acknowledged a greeting from his mother in the kitchen.

Richie sat in the family room and waited for Sophia. He switched on the TV but did not focus on the evening local drama series. He reflected over Sophia's plan to return to work in July, before he concluded that she would not, reckoning that she would simply be too occupied with the baby to think of going back to work. But just in case she did, he decided he would take his leave in July to stay home with the baby, and their house staff.

"Ooh no." Richie said on remembering what his father had said - after six months of probation he would go through an interview to prove that he was qualified to be the director of Africa Markets & Money Exchange.

Richie knew what that meant, he would have to put in extra effort at work in the coming six months. How would he achieve that when Sophia was determined that they relocate to their own house at about the same time?

Sophia walked past Richie and into the kitchen, where she met Patience who was leaving the kitchen.

"I made your favourite soup, you may take it now. That way, you will have enough space for dinner in the next hour."

Sophia followed Patience to the dining room.

Richie followed them. "I see Mum does not want me to enjoy some of your soup, I'm off to meet with Sam." He patted Sophia on the shoulder. "I will be back soon, that's if I convince Sam to join us for dinner."

Sam was Richie's age-mate and cousin, the youngest son of a younger brother of Mwasimba. Sam's father died when he was barely two years old.

Though Sam's father had developed a fresh flower export business, Mwasimba paid school fees for the children of his deceased brother. Sam ended up attending the same primary and secondary schools as Richie before proceeding to Malaysia for his university education. Since his return, four years ago, he had fully immersed himself in the family's cut-flower business, relieving his mother from the demanding position of manager.

Richie walked outside, towards the car garage.

Chapter 32

By the time the kitchen staff wheeled food to the dining room, Sophia had asked questions and received detailed responses from Patience.

When Sophia verbalized her fear of how she would spend the remaining six weeks before the baby's arrival, Patience enumerated a list of things she needed to do by January. The weekly visits by her masseuse would now increase to two or three times a week. The same person would also walk with her in the mornings, to avoid the intense afternoon sunshine as the December-February hot-and-dry-season set in.

Her visits to the doctor would increase from bi-weekly to weekly, or whenever needed.

"Why Mum? So many visits, yet I am not sick."

"The visits are recommended by many medical practitioners for the wellbeing of mother and child. No need to panic." Patience said.

Patience added. "The visits are normal, especially nowadays, as many women delay pregnancy into their thirties and beyond. Not you of course. Your category could be of young women joining the workforce, reducing the physical activities they are routinely involved in."

Sophia sipped more soup as Patience added. "The other item to think about is your hair. Would you like it to stay open or braided?"

Sophia lifted her left hand and touched her hair, combed back, resting on her shoulders. "I will have it braided. I am told that I will get terribly busy once the baby arrives, though I do not see with what new duties?"

Patience smiled, concluding that Sophia did not know how busy babies made new mothers. Patience hoped that Sophia would get so busy after the baby arrived that she would voluntarily resign from work and stay permanently home.

Not wanting to confess that she was eager to see Sophia stop working, Patience said, "It varies with individuals. Between your body needing a lot of food and rest to recover well, and the baby needing to breastfeed, there will not be much time left."

Sophia smiled, prompting Patience to add. "You might even surprise yourself by asking for an extension of your maternity leave. The company is renowned for permitting women to take up to one year of maternity leave."

"I have my doubts that I will need more time to sleep once the baby is born. All I am waiting for is the day of delivery, and thereafter have my past energy back."

To Sophia, there was no way a baby would occupy her entire day. Growing up she had seen her mother pause from regular housework long enough for a child to breastfeed before she resumed her tasks.

Sophia wondered what else she would be doing after bathing, breastfeeding, and singing a lullaby to send the baby to sleep. She would perhaps spend the extra time reading books, newspapers, journals and checking the Internet for information on global financial markets. That way, she would be up to date with new happenings, and remain adequately informed to engage in discussions with Richie.

She held onto the dining table and heaved herself out of the chair as the house phone rang. "I will get that since I am already on my feet." She answered the phone, uttering many okays before she replaced the receiver and proceeded to the toilet.

"That was Richie, asking us to eat all the food. Your boys are at Bill's house, and from the background noise, there must be a large crowd having a lot of fun." Sophia said when back to the dining room.

At 9:00p.m., Sophia excused herself, "I need to go sleep if I am to have energy for church tomorrow."

"Our God is an understanding God. If you feel tired, stay home, say your Sunday prayers in your heart. Sometimes they are better that way."

"You've convinced me, though I wonder what I will do the rest of the day."

"You can sleep more in the morning. Join us at the club in the afternoon, for one or two hours."

"Sounds like what I will do. Good night Mum," Sophia said as she walked away.

Patience watched her as she took short and slow steps until she disappeared past the family room.

Patience was happy that Sophia had agreed to join them at the club. It had been many weeks since they were at the club together. She wanted more of her friends to see Sophia, especially those not aware that the Mwasimba finally had a grandchild on the way.

Chapter 33

Richie met with Enock and Sam at their local shopping center where Enock joined Richie in his car for their drive to Bill's house.

Twenty minutes later, Richie parked his car in the driveway of Bill's house. He was surprised at the amount of noise, both from the music and from the dozen or so men at the back of the house.

As Richie parked his car in front of Sam's car, he saw Bill walking their direction. Bill shook Enock's hand while patting him on the shoulder. "Thanks for bringing my lost brother here."

Sam parked his car and joined the trio. "You now understand the reason I am still single," Sam said as he turned to Enock. "These married men stick to their wives like glue, before you add babies along the way."

They all laughed while walking to join the rest of the group at the barbeque.

Enock nudged Sam. "You might find yourself the odd one out next year. Richie introduced me to a gem. All I need are ideas on how to win her heart."

The four men stopped without prompting and looked at Richie who in turn scanned each of them. "Why have you stopped? She is not comparable to mine. Mine is the best."

Sam held Richie by the arm. "What am I hearing? That you bypassed me, the older one, and gave a nice lady to Enock?"

"There is no way you can have Sophia's sister. The elders will make us their special case, asking for a lime-green goat, and more… for cleansing purposes," Richie explained.

"Aaah," Sam sighed loudly.

"You are revealing the identity before I gather the courage to approach her, to ask her to be my girlfriend?" Enock cautioned Richie.

"Take your time and you will have only yourself to blame," Richie said to Enock before he turned to Bill. "You have a new case here. Do you recommend daily roses on her office-desk, evening tea, or first-class tickets to fashion shows in Europe?"

As the new arrivals found seats and made themselves comfortable, Michael, who had all along not left his position at the barbeque, called out, "Did we forget someone on the trip to fashion week? I can ask Beauta to turn the plane back," he said while shoving his left hand into his trouser pocket. He retrieved his cell phone.

Enock thundered. "We prefer that you focus on the meat. We are hungry," as he walked over to greet the half-dozen men who had not left their seats.

Richie and Sam joined in the greeting.

Enock scanned the seated men. "I see a lot of bachelors here. Richie, no more mentions of my girl here." He turned back to the men. "I see three cheetahs that might run faster than me, and I see two lions that could swallow her whole."

As the men broke into laughter, Enock picked up a paper plate and went to Michael. "I need all the cooked meat, a gift for Richie, for leaving the side of his wife, and, to thank him for directing me to some cutie, a potential girlfriend."

It was long past two in the morning when Richie returned home. Not wanting to disturb Sophia from her sleep, he tiptoed into the bathroom and showered.

Before he got into bed, he posted a note on the bathroom door. "Hi Sunshine, I had fun with the boys. Hope you don't mind if I skip church tomorrow." He was certain Sophia would see the note on her way to use the toilet many times before the morning sunrise.

Sophia read the note at around five in the morning. She took a pencil and wrote on top of Richie's message, "That makes two of us."

Chapter 34

Like previous company celebrations preceding the Christmas break, that year's celebration was spectacular.

All one could say was that the parties by the Mwasimba Group of Companies only got better with time. Invitations had gone out to both company collaborators and competitors, and to the newly recruited members of the Africa Markets & Money Exchange.

Sophia stayed at home, aware that had she attended the party, she would not have stayed for more than an hour, which would have made Richie feel obliged to leave the party with her.

Richie attended the party and mostly engaged in discussions with whoever asked him about AMME. He was more optimistic on seeing company representatives from four of the firms he had visited in South Africa and Uganda. Their presence made him even more hopeful that AMME would quickly pick up momentum. He promised himself that the following year he would travel to more countries to recruit more members.

At around midnight, guests started to leave the party. Richie stayed on for another hour to meet and chat with some relatives, friends, and acquaintances from the various clubs in the city.

There were a few notably well-dressed people in an array of vintage Chanel dresses, Maki Oh separates that were wonderfully and ironically easy to spot. Some of the ladies from the clubs were clad in too much Prada.

Richie caught himself severally either yawning or staring at his Rolex before he decided it was time to go reunite with Sophia. On the drive home he was glad that he had only ten working days before he started his month-long leave in January.

He had consciously decided to work the whole of December though the office closed officially on the 20th of December to reopen on the second day of January. He would then transfer his December holidays worked to January, so as to be with Sophia on her countdown to the birth of their baby in mid-January. He did not relish the idea of being still at work by the time a phone call came through announcing the birth of his first-born child. He planned to be present with Sophia at every stage.

As the driver waited patiently in the long queue of vehicles leaving the party premises, Richie's mind wandered off, thinking about how he would spend each day in the first two weeks of January.

He reflected on how it had taken him many months of unsuccessful attempts to get Sophia to resign from her job. He thought of the many pleasant surprises Sophia had of late thrown at him. She had made decisions without consulting him, yet the decisions were practical and to his liking. He recalled the many occasions when they had had their arguments. He also recalled the happy moments. All the moments had made him love Sophia more. She challenged him to reflect further on issues he rarely thought of.

The many moments they spent together helped him realize how much Sophia loved him. Except for her fear of not having a job or earning her money, she liked her married life. She loved her family and his family.

Richie laughed out loudly on remembering that Sophia and Patience had so far developed a mother-daughter relationship, were good friends, thus doing away with his earlier fear of dreaded mother-in-law and daughter-in-law conflicts.

Richie dozed off as the driver meandered out of the parking of the club and drove the short distance to join the main road. He woke up as they traversed the fairly deserted stretch of city roads. He wondered what would happen if he started to consult more with his wife before making decisions that concerned their family.

The gates to the Mwasimba compound swung open and they drove inside. Richie nodded to the saluting night watchmen.

He made a promise to himself, to consult Sophia more often, seeking for her opinion, especially now that some of the decisions she made had brought him much joy. Like the decision to begin her maternity leave earlier.

He opened the front door to the house. As the sensor lights shooed away the darkness, he looked around and wondered if he had become like his father, working hard in the office, and making decisions he considered good for his family. He murmured, "The biggest difference is that Sophia cannot be like my mother. I must learn to treat her differently."

Unlike the other days when Richie would tiptoe into the bedroom to avoid waking Sophia, he entered and woke her up, fully aware that three in the morning was not a time for many people to want to be awoken.

~~~~~~

Richie was happy with their early morning conversation where he asked questions and let Sophia share her thoughts first before he voiced his.

Sophia informed Richie that an evening spent alone in the house, except for some brief company from Theresa, had helped her make better plans for their future. She had decided that a one-year maternity leave would be more ideal, giving her enough time to breastfeed the baby in the first six months, and more time to wean the baby while they prepared to move to their house.

Richie was very happy with her decision on the one-year maternity leave, though he would have preferred to hear her say she would resign from work.

Deep down in his heart, Richie learned something - that consulting, at whatever level, made a significant and positive difference.

They slept at the first rays of the morning sun, at 5:30am. Richie fell asleep a happy man. He foresaw an
~~~~~~

entire year ahead, of him working hard at the office, while Sophia stayed home with their baby. One year would afford him enough time to focus on the demanding activities of AMME, seeing him qualify to be Director of the new department, with adequate earnings to fully provide for his family.

Chapter 35

Sophia took long to believe she was holding a baby in her hands, her own baby.

Richie had not left her side since they arrived at the hospital and checked into the VIP wing, almost twenty-four hours earlier.

She was thankful… nay, grateful, that her life could hardly get any better. She loved being married and was happy that she was embarking on a one-year maternity leave.

Before she could reflect further, the door to her private room opened, and Patience walked in.

Richie tilted his head in the direction of his mother. His lips parted, like he wanted to say something, alert her that her loud prayer could wake the baby from sleep.

Before Richie could utter a word, Sophia fidgeted and pulled a bed sheet over her chest on seeing Beauta and Georgina walk into the room.

Beauta placed a beautiful bouquet of fresh flowers on the side table while Georgina placed a teddy bear and a card on the same table.

Beauta kissed Sophia on both cheeks and then the baby on the forehead. "Well done. You have opened the door for us."

The End

One last request

Reviews help potential readers to find books. If you enjoyed reading this book, please go to Amazon and leave a few sentences on what you liked about the book.

Thank you.

Book three, **Trapped Inside the Family Box** is available for you to read.

Be among the first to know when the author publishes another book. Go to EileenOmosa.com and join the growing list of my fans. Thank you for your support.

About the Author

K is for Kwamboka

Eileen K. Omosa, Ph.D., writes novels on change and adaptation. She applies knowledge and skills gained from over fifteen years of work experience in the natural resources management sector in Africa. She has facilitated projects on conflict management, forestry, and food security, mainstreaming gender into natural resources management, land tenure and access rights for sustainable livelihoods, among other topics.

Eileen grew up in rural Kenya until the day she packed that grey suitcase for the city to pursue university education, and she has never stopped traveling the world. On her way to the North Pole, she made a long stopover in Canada where she attained a PhD in Rural and Environmental Sociology.

Since 2016, she has published nine contemporary romance novels set in Africa. The novels will get you reflective on development-related issues, including, if education opens more doors or conflicts for the African woman, and if the women ever find a balance between career and cultural expectations? She follows immigrants to their destinations and explores how they establish and maintain romantic relationships in their new country.

When Eileen is not at her writing desk, she will be found outdoors implementing research on household food security, the reason she cultivates vegetables in her city. Visit her online at EileenOmosa.com

Books by the Author

An African Woman's Journey Series

1. Ignited by Education
2. Slowed by a Baby
3. Trapped Inside the Family Box
4. The Housegirl Becoming Angela
5. Dare to Marry a Billionaire's Daughter
6. The Enemy's Daughter
7. An African Woman's Journey Boxset 1

An Immigrant's Marriage Series:

1. The Fear Within Us
2. The Family Between Us
3. The Love Within Us (2021)

Below is a preview of the novels

Book 1: Ignited by Education

Sophia is at the peak of her career when society interrupts to remind her she's at the ripe age for marriage?

A contemporary women's fiction for those who believe that genuine love, when nurtured well, will result in the right decisions to conquer external challenges. The road to happiness in life involves twists and turns, intersections, and gives and takes—the place where Sophia Mariko finds herself.

Sophia does not need a reminder that her used-clothes' business is not enough to pay school fees for her siblings. When she receives a letter of employment six months after graduation, she vows to shun romance, which she terms as a distraction from her career goals. But that's until her father summons her to the village to get married.

She could resist and stay in the city, but her job is insecure. Richie floods her work desk with red roses and proposes to her. Sophia turns his overtures down but becomes desperate on learning he's the son of her employer. She's aware of the Company's rule on a romance between employees, one of them must resign.

How will Sophia choose? Can she run away from marriage, yet her upbringing prepared her for the role of a wife and mother? Or will she abandon her job and drop back into the poverty she has worked so hard to overcome?

Ignited by Education is book one in An African Woman's Journey Series. Sophia's story continues in Slowed by a Baby and concludes in The Woman She Became.

Book 3: Trapped Inside the Family Box

Can Sophia transition into her new family without sacrificing something personal?

Sophia and Richie leave their baby behind and go for a holiday to celebrate Richie's promotion at work and to prepare for Sophia's imminent return to work. Little did she know the journey would transform her career and family life.

While in the USA, Richie reconnects with James, his long-gone brother, but fails to convince him to return home. Sophia steps in and persuades James, unaware of the momentous favour she's done Richie's family. Did she get too busy to mind her well-being?

Sophia becomes reflective on what it means to lead a happy and satisfactory life, the kind she envisioned. She finds the answer and realizes she's always had it on her long journey of searching for empowerment and social change.

Does she welcome the WOMAN she's become?

Trapped Inside the Family Box is book three in An African Women's Journey Series. Sophia's story starts in The Girl who Left the Village, followed by Slowed by a Baby. A trilogy where education, culture, ambition, and love intertwine.

Book 4: The House girl Becoming Angela

Angela cannot afford to lose this job of house girl to Ronny's children, no matter what his sister or mother-in-law say or do. But can she change her title to Wife?

Ronny Kipchoge's well-balanced domestic sphere tilts, rendering him a single parent to three young children. One year of residing with his parents gives him the child-care support he needs to perform his CEO tasks. But now he must leave for his house, give his mother time to care for his ailing father. Schools will reopen in two weeks; the reason Ronny has no patience when his sister interrupts him with her criteria on why he should not hire Angela as the nanny for his children.

Angela desperately needs a job to provide for her son and save for her lifelong dream of a university education. While Ronny fumbles through grief and work, Angela, his twenty-three-year-old nanny, "mothers" his children so well that he has ideas on how to make her stay forever. But the more Ronny tries, the more he draws Angela into a web of struggles at his house, as friends and family are eager to get Angela out of the picture.

Will Ronny and Angela let outsiders dampen the growing attraction between them, or can they combine forces to overcome the challenges and live a HEA in this clean second chance romance?

Book 5: Dare to Marry a Billionaire's Daughter

He's hesitant of women from wealthy families, she terrified of marrying to please her parents. But when their paths cross at a gym, can they resist their hearts' desires in this forbidden romance?

Odhiambo, a gym instructor, has sworn off women from affluent families after his fiancée was taken away to marry a well-off man. When he's hired to help Redempta shape into a centerpiece at her unavoidable wedding, he senses trouble. The moment he extends a hand to welcome her into the gym, a warm tingle runs up his spine, only arrested by Cynthia's scowl. He dismisses the feeling—nothing can work between him and Redempta.

Nyawira is focused on her career when Cynthia reminds her, she's running out of time to get married. Turning down the wealthy men chosen for her is tough, but nothing compared to telling her mother she's in love with her gym trainer, and Odhiambo is in debt.

When Nyawira and Odhiambo dine at a location of the city Cynthia would not approve of, her body, mind, and taste buds awaken. She's in love with Odhiambo and he wants to take the risk, again. Now Odhiambo must decide if it's worth the trouble to marry a billionaire's daughter when he's in debt?

This book is for you if you've been looking for a clean contemporary romance on what it takes to marry across the tracks.

Book 6: Dare to Marry the Enemy's Son

What if she returns home with the man she cannot live without, and her parents cannot live with?

Bonuke Kebaso has envisioned a career in the solar industry as the way to gain independence from her parents. Determined to complete her university study program, she forgoes her comfort in the city for field research at a solar farm in a remote area of Maasai Mara. Everything is going according to plan, until a helicopter lands and Jade, the son of her father's enemy, jogs down the ladder.

Jade Momina has lived his adult life driving flashy cars in Nairobi. But when he calls off his arranged marriage and becomes the front-page story in the media, his father gives him one option—run, get busy at a family road construction project until the media find their next popular story. Bad press will crumble Momina's success as a politician and business owner. When the helicopter lands, Jade pauses long enough to rest a hand on his pounding heart, thankful. If the person he sees beyond the dusty airstrip is Letitiah, he's ready to forgive his father for banishing him to Maasai Mara.

The sensible action for Bonuke is to call her father to airlift her back to Nairobi. But she will not, completing the field study is her only means to financial freedom from her parents, and seeing Jade only reminds her of their stolen kiss nine years ago. Three months at a remote work site rekindles her feelings, and she falls into Jade's open arms.

Can the two lovebirds overpower the combined forces of their feuding families to live a HEA in this clean contemporary romance?

Manufactured by Amazon.ca
Bolton, ON